HORIZON BETA

HORIZON BETA

D. W. VOGEL

Horizon Beta

Future House Publishing

Text © 2020 Wendy Vogel

ISBN: 978-1-950020-01-0

Developmental editing by Abbie Robinson
Substantive editing by Emma Hoggan
Copy editing by Stephanie Cullen
Interior design by Amanda LaFrance

This book is for Andrew, who has saved my
life twice now.

CAPTAIN'S PERSONAL JOURNAL

VOYAGE YEAR 158

I think we're going to make it.

The Horizon Beta has been trouble since the day she launched. The drive system has failed nineteen times in this journey, and we've scavenged every millimeter, stealing from every non-life support system we can to keep her running. Omicron Eridani was a pipe dream. We never would have made it. Everyone on board this ship owes their lives to Captain Crowder's decision to change course. Epsilon Eridani was light-years closer. Fifty years later, I would have made the same call. We're nearly there, but even at our current range, we aren't sure there's an atmosphere to support us. She may have aimed us at a dead hunk of rock.

But it's our only chance.

And I think we'll get there mostly in one piece.

Measuring in Earth years, we are currently about three years away from the planet. Three years until we find out if the five hundred souls entrusted to my care will have a chance at a new life on a new planet, or are doomed to die on a generational colony ship, forever orbiting a lifeless world.

VOYAGE YEAR 161

The stars have guided us to safety.

This will be my last entry as captain of the Horizon Beta. In just a few hours, we will leave what remains of our ship for good. Epsilon Eridani will be the new home of the remnant of humanity that made this journey, generation after generation hoping to one day reach a planet like this.

We entered low orbit this morning and launched the probes. The atmosphere is higher in oxygen than we're used to, but we will adapt soon enough. There are saltwater oceans, and freshwater streams coming down off rocky mountains. Our away team returned with samples, and our scanners tell us we are biocompatible with much of the plant life, which means there will be food for us to forage safely while we set up our colony and plant our own seeds, brought from the vaults of our lost home world. Our sensors show plenty of insects to pollinate them. We'll also take down some of the huge vats of algae that have sustained us through this endless journey. Personally, if I never have to eat another meal of blue-green algae, it will be soon enough.

Surely this is a new Eden, a paradise where humanity can thrive.

We have launched all the satellites safely. So as long as our technology survives, we will have access to all the data stored on the Beta's systems. Everything we need will be at our fingertips, and by the time the equipment we take from the Beta wears out, we should be well on our way to our own industrial society.

Everything has gone according to plan. My ship will be the last to leave. Once everything we need has been ferried down to the planet's surface, I'll be the final soul on the Horizon Beta, engaging the autopilot. When I depart, she'll be empty forever. There will be no reason to return.

She may not last long in orbit, and I worry for our satellites. We had to fly through a thick debris field to get here. The asteroid band is very close to the planet, and without a living pilot to guide her, there's a good chance that the Beta and our satellites might be destroyed sooner than we like. But we'll survive without them.

The first of our transports has departed. The first of our people are about to do what no human has done for a hundred and sixty-one years: stand on the living soil of a real planet.

I've done it. I've brought our people to safety.

Along with all the captains before me, the Horizon Beta has brought us to sanctuary among the stars.

CHAPTER 1

NOAH

I lined up with the other boys, heart pounding in excitement. *Today's the day!*

Eight of us boys were ready for the Ranking. Over the next three days, our fates would be sealed.

The Master directed us in the elegant, clicking language they used to speak to us. Among ourselves we spoke the Lowform, but I was particularly adept at making the clicking noises. That had to count for something. Surely my ability to converse with them would be a leg up in the Ranks.

I could tell them apart, though they had no need for names. The Masters were all one mind, one great "We." They shared each other's thoughts, and if one fell, another rose into its place. We Lowforms had no such power. We were individuals, alone in the world. We had names given to us by our mothers, that group of females living deep in the tunnels, surrounded by crying babies and screaming toddlers. I hadn't been back to the Mothers' Hall since the Masters came for me over ten years ago. Since then I'd lived in the boys' area, where we learned the skills we would need once we were Ranked.

The clicks of the Master brought me to attention. I looked up past its huge pincers and into the expressionless, hard brown face.

"Running. White Rock. Return. Run fast."

Oh, I would. I would run fast.

I stood next to my best friend Chen, sweating in the morning humidity.

"Man, Noah. I wish we had diving today," he muttered. "Too hot to run."

I laughed. It was always too hot to run. But that's what the Masters wanted.

"This is the Ranking. Just do it," I said.

He would do his best. We all would. The prize for the chosen few demanded it.

I squinted across the low field. Anything could be hiding in those grasses. But the Masters were there to protect us. Without their great, stinging tails, we Lowforms were at risk from all the other insects that buzzed, hopped, crawled, and flew over the dry, cracked land to the soft sand where the ocean rolled in crashing waves. None of us felt entirely safe outside the thick mud walls our Masters built, the huge, towering Hive that sheltered us all. But the wind in my hair lifted my thoughts away from the dangers that lurked outside the Hive. It was time to run.

With two sharp clicks, we were off. My feet pounded on the hard ground, heels driving into the clay. White Rock was an outcropping in the distance, far across the grassy plain that separated our towering Hive from the green mountains beyond the plain. Between the rock and the mountains lay the Forbidden Zone, but we would turn back before we reached it. The first few steps I ran in the welcome shadow of the Hive, but soon it was left behind and the morning sun beat against my bare back. The cloth I wore around my waist flapped in the wind of my speed.

My mind raced as I ran. I didn't want to win the race, but I thought coming in second or third might be best. The winner was certain to get Ranked as a Runner, one of the Lowforms that accompanied the Master Soldiers on their patrols, bringing back messages to the Hive or scouting around. Runners didn't live long. The few I saw in my training always looked haggard, thin and ropey, eyes darting around all the time. I admired their service to the Hive, but I didn't want to be one. Too dangerous out there.

I was in front of the pack, cruising through the grassland, bare feet swishing along. My eyes scanned the high grass around me, alert for danger. Workers kept this path cut short, but anything could hide in the tall field around me.

A sharp elbow knocked me off my stride and I stumbled, crashing off the path and into the tall stalks. Gil shot past me, laughing.

"Did you fall? So sorry!" He skittered away down the corridor while I picked myself up off the ground. A couple of leaf-eaters had hopped onto my legs and I brushed them away before they could bite me, stumbling out into the short grass as the rest of the boys pounded past. Chen was at the back of the pack and I loped along next to him. He was breathing hard, sweat pouring off his face.

"I . . . saw . . . it," he panted. "He . . . pushed . . . you."

"He did," I answered. "It's okay. Don't wanna be Runner."

But I didn't want to lose any of the events in the Ranking. I was a great swimmer. Everybody said I was a shoo-in for Diver, whether in the dark, clear water that flowed in rivers under the Hive or in the sea where the waves beat the shore. Diver would be a great life for me. I'd be happy as a Diver.

Even if I came in last on this footrace, I could still be a Diver. But if I came in second or maybe third, the door would still be open. The shining door that led to the highest honor the Masters could bestow. I had dreamed about it for years. Only the very best were granted the title, and I wanted it so bad I could taste it.

Queen's Servant.

Every Ranking, the very best boys were taken into the depths of the Hive, to the secret, forbidden tunnels that led to the Queen herself. No other Lowforms ever got to see her. I couldn't imagine the glory of it. The Queen of the whole Hive. If I became her Servant, I'd get to see her. I'd be sent on some mission with her blessing, or remain in her chambers as her trusted protector, or . . . I didn't know, really. I'd never seen a Queen's Servant after they were chosen. They were far too exalted to return to the rest of us Lowforms. But maybe, just maybe, if I did well enough, I could join those ranks.

I grinned at Chen and poured on the speed.

CHAPTER 2

NOAH

I paused at the White Rock, panting. Beyond lay the Forbidden Zone, where only the Masters patrolled. It was a long, low, tree-lined valley dotted with huge shapes, long and unnatural. Parts of the huge shapes glinted in the afternoon sun, but most of them were brown and green, overgrown with creeping tendrils that waved in the hot breeze. A few Masters scuttled over the enormous growths, and I caught my breath for a moment, until a few of the other boys caught up with me. Then I was off again, sprinting back toward the Hive, lungs burning as my legs pumped.

Gil won the race. I came in third, behind the boy we all called Red because his skin turned scarlet every time he was out in the sun. He was bright red now, huffing and panting, but standing tall before the Masters.

"Race stop," the Master clicked. "This one fastest."

Gil beamed at the Master, and shot a wicked smile my way.

My blood pumped hot and I wanted to slug him, but Chen grabbed my arm. "Not worth it. Let him go be a Runner. Good riddance."

I smiled a little at that. Chen was right. It would be great to be rid of Gil.

"Hey, Noah," Gil said as he sauntered past. "You okay? Saw that fall. Right into the leaf-eaters. Tough luck."

My hands balled into fists, but once again, Chen was there.

"You sure are fast, Gil," he said. "Bet you'll be the fastest Runner ever."

Gil puffed up at that, glancing back to make sure the Masters had heard Chen's words.

They didn't deign to respond, of course. Such Low chatter was beneath them.

The Masters were magnificent in the late morning sun. It glinted off their armored backs, on the long, segmented tail with its stinger. Their six hind legs effortlessly ate the distance, and when they reared back to gesture at us with their huge pincers, we all shrank back. Next to them, we were nothing. Soft skin with no armor. Hideous hair growing from our heads. The fact that they allowed us to live in their Hive, to dive for their food and clean up their waste and maybe, just maybe, serve their Queen was unfathomable to me.

We plodded on our pathetic two legs down to the beach, surrounded by Master Soldiers. Past the towering brown Hive, we clambered down the rocky shore to where the ocean rolled in from so far away I couldn't see the end. The sun was high now, glittering off the distant waves. Rocks gave way to brown sand, soft and shifting under our ungainly feet. The Masters skittered right over it. Hot wind brought a salty, fishy smell. This cove was bordered on each side by rock formations that jutted straight into the sea, blocking the heaviest waves. With each passing wave, I glanced up and down the long, smooth beach, watching for the little bubbles that indicated a shellfish had burrowed into the sand.

The Masters loved shellfish.

But the Masters didn't swim. Far out beyond the breakers were vast fields of shellfish, lined up along hard coral ridges. They were deep underwater, and had to be pried loose with a tool, but I had mastered the technique. I was a great diver. This was my chance to shine.

"Dive," one clicked. "Here. Most food best."

One of the Masters had used a front limb to carve deep grooves into the sand, making large round circles, one for each of us. We would have a set amount of time until they called an end to collect as many shellfish as we could and place them in our circle. I grabbed a woven bag and tied it around my waist, handing another bag to Chen. Some of the boys weren't good swimmers. Chen wasn't. Instead of diving, he'd likely comb the sandy beach, watching for those bubbles and digging up the smaller shells as he could. He was pretty fast at it and would probably do fairly well. Gil wasn't a great ocean swimmer, either, so Chen would have to watch his back. A pile of the strong metal rods we used to harvest the shells sat next to the circles, and I tucked one into the rope holding the bag around my waist.

The Master clicked the signal, and off we went. I bolted

for the ocean, loping with huge strides into the oncoming waves. I dived under the largest ones, keeping my forward motion as the sea tried to shove me back toward land. As soon as I was out far enough, I submerged and swam, kicking with strong strokes away from the breaker line, out to the depth. The sea was alive with fish, darting among huge rock formations on which scuttled a hundred different kinds of sea-insects, brightly colored and shimmering under the weak sunlight.

The shellfish that the Masters loved were anchored to the rocks on the beach side of the cove. Shoals of them ran in long lines parallel to the sea's edge, opening their shells to suck in seawater and closing them when a shadow passed overhead.

I scouted a likely area, dove down to grab a large rock, and kicked to the surface.

Breathe out, one, two, three. The breath whooshed out of me as I squeezed my chest.

One huge breath in, and down we go. The rock I had taken helped pull me down when the air in my lungs tried to stop my descent. Head down, I pinched my nose and pumped air into my head so my ears didn't burn.

Once on the bottom I set to work. Pulling the pry rod from my waist, I braced myself against the sharp rocks. My hands were long since toughened to leather, and the edges didn't cut me like they had when I was first learning to dive almost ten years ago. My rhythm took over. *Dig the rod in. Lever out the shell. Peel it off the rocks. Stuff it in the bag. Repeat.*

I harvested until my chest screamed for air. Grabbing another rock, I kicked for the surface. When my head broke,

I sucked in a huge gasp of air, holding my face clear of the rolling waves. A quick glance at the shore showed distant figures rushing along the waterline, grabbing at shells in the surf. I couldn't tell who was who, or how well they were doing.

Back down we go. Breathe out, one, two, three.

After three trips down to the shell field, my bag bulged. Time to head in and dump. I had no idea when the Masters might call a halt to the test. The older Divers I trained with had varying accounts of their own Ranking. Some only had time to get a single trip, while others were diving all afternoon, until their heads and ears were pounding from the pressure. The Masters were clever and would always bring out our best.

Waves pounded into my back as I found footing in the shallows and lurched toward dry land. Chen was up on the beach, dumping a bagful of the smaller shells from the tide line into his circle. I jogged up the beach, pulling at the rope that tied my bag shut, clanking with sharp seashells around my legs. When I emptied the bag into my circle, I could see that I was in the lead so far. My pile was the biggest, but not by much.

Get back out there. Win this.

I turned and headed back to the sea with a glance at the Masters. Their faces had no expression, hard plates shining in the sun. Their chests bellowed rhythmically, slow and calm under the hot sun. My own chest was heaving, but I could rest later. *Win this.*

White foam tickled my legs as my feet slapped into the water. I turned back one last time to make sure the Masters hadn't called a halt.

A figure was in my circle, crouching over my pile of shells. The boy grabbed a large handful and scuttled over to his own circle, dropping them inside before trotting down toward the water.

Zero doubt who had stolen my shells.

Gil. And the Masters had watched it happen.

My face heated up, neck burning with rage. He took my shells. They watched him take my shells.

Was this some kind of test? Of course it was. The Masters were far above caring about the petty squabbles of Lowforms. Why would they care if someone cheated? Only results mattered.

Gil trotted down the water's edge where Chen was bent over, digging out a shell. He shoved hard into the smaller boy's side as he passed, and Chen toppled over onto the wet sand.

My hands were pulling the pry rod from my waist before I knew I was running.

"Hey, that's it!" I shouted. "You're a thief and a dung-scraper. I saw you take my shells."

Gil whipped around and saw me coming, pry bar raised over my head.

"Noah, no!" Chen's voice barely reached my ears through the white-hot anger pulsing in my head. He tried to grab at me as I flew past him toward Gil, who had turned to run but gotten his feet mired in wet sand. Gil toppled over and Chen grabbed my arm. The prybar fell from my hand and I fell onto Gil, fists flying.

Neither of us could get purchase in the wet, sticky sand, but I caught him a solid blow right in the nose. Crimson blood streamed out and his eyes got huge and round. He rolled his weight on top of me and reared back to punch me, but Chen launched into him from behind. Both boys crashed into me and someone's knee drove the air right out of my lungs.

"Stop! Stop! The Masters said it's over!" The other boys crowded around us, pulling us apart.

I couldn't get air. My chest wouldn't rise and I lay there on the sand as wave after wave rushed up around me. Chen pulled me up to a sitting position and slowly my chest relaxed, allowing a trickle of air in.

"Noah, what were you doing? He just knocked me over. That's just Gil. He's always been a dung-scraper."

I shook my head. "Took my shells." Words came in quick gasps. "Saw him." *Breathe.* "Masters saw it."

Chen looked up the beach to where the Masters watched the rest of the boys gathering up our harvest. "Why would they let him do that?"

I shrugged. "They just want shells."

He helped me to my feet and I retrieved the prybar from where it had fallen into the sand. My whole back was gritty. There was sand in my hair, in my clothes, ground between my toes. I took a moment to wade into deeper water and rinse off before joining Chen and the rest of the boys up the beach.

Gil was holding his nose, tipping his head back. His whole chin was red, and where he'd touched his chest, the skin was smeared with his blood.

Good. Deserves it.

I didn't win diving, but even with Gil's treachery, I was a solid second. Chen was right in the middle, which should be pretty safe. Gil won, but there was no way they'd pick him as a Diver. They wanted a shellfish harvest, and although he proved he could steal them, he hadn't proved he could collect them. My dream was still alive.

My stomach growled. I picked up one of the bags of shells and joined the party carrying them toward the Hive.

By the time we got the harvest turned over to the Masters in the Hive, the sun had disappeared behind the bulk of our enormous home. Built by the Masters over a hundred generations, it was a masterpiece. Mud hardened to solid rock, smooth brown on the outside, but on the inside the warren of hallways was as intricate as any spiraling seashell that washed up on the beach. Branching corridors led away from each other, crisscrossed, and doubled back, twisting ever downward. The higher levels allowed the Masters to survey the surrounding area, breathing in the world for miles. Our Queen owned every bit of land that could be seen from the topmost lookout of the Hive, from the ocean's shore north and south along the coast, all the way through the grasslands to the green mountains and beyond. There had once been enemies on our land, other Hives ruled by inferior Queens. Our Soldiers destroyed them, and their Hives lay empty. We were victorious in battle every time. How lucky were we to live in the greatest Hive that ever was?

"Did you see it?" Chen startled me out of my reverie as we grabbed baskets, filled them with stones that had sat out in the sun all day, and entered the cool comfort of the Hive.

"See what?" I rubbed my ribs, sore where Gil had kicked me in our fight.

"The Feral."

We followed the rest of the boys into the tunnels, heading for food. The stones in our baskets glowed with a clean, green light as we passed through the dark portions of the corridors. The walls were rough and brown, with holes to the sunlight at regular intervals, the floor smooth from generations of Masters' feet, hard exoskeleton with delicate feelers all around, and our Lowform feet, soft and plodding.

"A Feral? You saw a Feral?" My eyes widened. "Where?"

"During the race outside. Didn't you see it?"

Chen and I lined up behind the rest of the boys at one of the outer chambers on ground level. It had been specially formed at ground level as an annex to the Hive, with a lattice of holes in the roof and walls. Inside sat three huge tubs. They were made of a material not found anywhere else in the Hive, but similar to what our prybars and some of the other tools we used were made of. It was hard and smooth, and cold to the touch. Metal.

"No. What did it look like?" I swung my bag of glowstones over my shoulder and grabbed a tightly woven bowl. From inside the cool tubs I scooped a bowlful of the green slimy soup that was most of our diet.

Chen grinned, already slurping the green soup from his bowl. "It was a male. Bigger than us, looked pretty old. It was hiding almost all the way to the rock." He wiped his mouth with the back of his arm. "You really didn't see it?"

I shook my head. "No. I was pretty mad, just trying to make up time."

A Master stood at the exit of the tub room with a basket of the shellfish we had collected. As we passed, each boy was allowed to take one. I cracked open the shell and sucked down the salty goodness, tossing the empty shell into another basket at the doorway. My bowl of green soup sloshed as I walked, heading down the slope toward the sleeping room.

Chen's soup was gone, and he dropped glowstones along our path, saving a few for our quarters when we got there. "I think it was alone. They usually are."

Ferals. So close to the Hive. I hadn't seen one for ages. They looked like us Lowforms, but they were not like us. They didn't live in the Hive, and because they served no Queen, they were wild and dangerous. They were one of the many perils the Masters protected us from when we ventured outside.

I shuddered. "I'm glad I didn't see it. I wonder what it was doing so close? Hope the Masters killed it."

We trooped down and down, past the fungus rooms where Masters and Lowforms tended the mushroom gardens, past the long hallway that led to the Mothers' chambers, where female Lowforms and their babies lived in the calm glow of the stones, protected from all the dangers above. We never went down that hallway. Masters guarded it, keeping our breeding females safe. I had been born somewhere down that hallway, to one of the females I had no memory of. When I was four years old, the Masters brought me out, never to return. Only mothers and babies were allowed in that area of the Hive, and I had no interest in going down there, anyway. Who would want to be around a bunch of babies?

I shuddered again, for a different reason. What if I failed

the Ranking? I hoped I'd be a Diver, spending every day of the rest of my life in the ocean prying up food, or down in the clear, cold rivers that flowed beneath the deepest tunnels of our Hives. I dared to dream I might possibly gain the highest honor and enter the Queen's Service. But what if I didn't? What if I got Ranked as a Gardener in the fungus garden, or a Cleaner, carrying out waste from Masters and Lowforms? Worst of all, what if they made me a Caretaker? I would spend the rest of my life in the Mothers' Hall, locked away with the females and screaming babies, never to see the sunlight again.

No, that couldn't possibly happen. I did well in the footrace, and I was second in Diving. Tomorrow was another swimming event, and I'd do well. I wasn't the strongest for the rock carrying challenge, but there was no way I'd get Ranked so low as to end up a Caretaker.

Chen and I found our sleeping room, a small alcove off one of the hallways. We bunked with four other boys, and mercifully Gil wasn't one of them. The Hive was chilly and the light from the remaining stones in our baskets cast long shadows up the walls. I was deep in the Hive, safe and protected. Whatever happened tomorrow, I'd be ready.

And by the end of the day, one way or another, my fate would be sealed.

CHAPTER 3

NOAH

We started the next morning with rock carrying. It was simple: move heavy stones from a giant pile into a marked-off area, just like the shellfish areas had been marked.

The stones were piled on the deep sand where the beach rose up to the high dunes. Tall seagrass bordered the upper edge of the sand, ending in a copse of trees that extended inland toward the distant hills. Cool wind blew in off the ocean, ruffling my hair as I lined up next to Chen.

Three Masters stood in front of the rock pile, all Soldiers. The largest one was a bright golden color. Another was more mottled brown, and the third had scars all along the plates of its left side. Bright morning sun threw their massive shadows onto the waving grasses at their backs.

The golden one clicked, gesturing with his pincers. "Get. Go. Drop. More."

It meant *pick up a stone, carry it over to the destination area, put it down, and repeat.* I stretched out my shoulders and cracked my neck. Ready to go.

The wind shifted and all three of the Soldiers tensed, feelers twitching. The two larger ones darted away into the seagrass, leaving the scarred Soldier behind.

"Stay," it clicked, and we all huddled together behind the rocks.

I peered out over the pile of stones. Over the top of the high grass, the raised tails of the two Master Soldiers slipped together into the trees.

"What's out there?" Chen whispered.

"Can't tell."

The Soldier guarding us clicked for silence.

I edged away from it around the other side of the rock pile. Our Soldiers were on the trail of something, and I didn't want to miss it.

A dark brown shape burst from the trees. It ran on two legs, and I could hear its ragged breathing as it lunged through the grass toward us. A Feral. Maybe the one Chen had seen yesterday, lurking near the Forbidden Zone when we raced to White Rock. It was taller than me, and its skin lighter. It had a thick beard and was wrapped in some kind of strange cloth, tight around its legs.

My mouth hung open as the creature ran straight toward us. I couldn't move, frozen in terror, my feet dug into the sand. Feral. They were dangerous. Everyone knew that. There was no threat our Soldiers couldn't protect us from, but of all the creatures that lurked in the forests, Ferals were the ones we feared most. We whispered stories about them in the night. If a Feral got into the Hive, it would kill all the children. They were stronger than us Lowforms, and they hated us because we were safe inside and they were left to the horrors of the outside world.

The Soldiers emerged from the trees behind it in hot pursuit.

Behind me, the rest of the boys scrambled backwards, but I was paralyzed by the sight of the thing heading right for me.

With a flip of its tail, the scarred Soldier knocked me out of the way, placing itself between me and the approaching Feral. I stumbled back and crouched low in the sand.

The creature skidded to a halt, surrounded by the three Soldiers.

It's all right. They won't let it get us.

With a terrifying shriek, the Feral lunged for me. I barely registered the motion as the scarred Soldier whipped its tail around, driving the thick barb into the creature's side. When it pulled the barb away, blood leaked from the hole it left.

The Feral dropped to its knees. In seconds, the venom from the Soldier would paralyze it, ending the threat to our Hive.

Sound gurgled from its throat. It almost sounded like words.

"You . . . you . . . we . . ."

Words. Ridiculous. The grunting noises ended as the venom took hold and the Feral collapsed in the sand.

The Soldiers parted and I got a better look at the creature. It looked just like a Lowform. Male. Older than anyone I'd ever known. His eyes were still moving, though the rest of his body was limp on the ground. His breathing was shallow and labored.

My heart swelled with pride. This monster had come to destroy us. If our Soldiers weren't so brave, he would have snuck into the Hive and killed all the babies in the Mothers' Hall deep in the tunnels. My skin was chilled in the warm air as I stared at him. The thing was heading straight for me. He would have killed me too, but our Soldiers protected me. They put themselves between me and the evil creature that lay on the ground before me. I hadn't even known he was out there, lying in wait.

The brown Soldier grabbed the Feral's arm in its pincer and dragged him through the sand, leaving a trench in the deep powder. His eyes rolled in his head. They locked onto mine as the Soldier dragged him past me, and another shiver raced down my back.

I watched the Soldier pull the thing all the way to the Hive, disappearing into the shadowy entrance.

Chen appeared by my side. He peered out toward the tree line. "Do you think there are more out there?"

I looked at the two remaining Soldiers grooming brambles off their legs. They paid no attention to us or to the forest behind them.

"No," I said. My shoulders relaxed and I sighed, my heart slowing back to normal. "They'd know if there were. Nothing's out there."

I grinned at him. "We're always safe with our Masters around."

CHAPTER 4

NOAH

The sun was hot on my back as I puffed along, rocks under each arm, feet slipping in the deep sand. After the terror of the Feral's attack, we still had to complete the rock-carrying event in the Ranking. I didn't win, and neither did Gil. Chen was one of the strongest, and finished in second place.

"Good job, buddy," I said, slapping him on the back. "Impressive."

He grinned and nodded, too out of breath to talk.

We followed the Masters back inside, down the spiraling tunnels to the very bottom of the Hive. The air got more damp as we descended, with brown mold on the walls. Our glow stones lit the way. *Maybe that's where Chen will end up.* It was someone's job to constantly renew the stones all over the Hive, taking out the spent ones to recharge in the sunlight and bringing down the ones that had absorbed enough light to illuminate the tunnels. The Masters didn't need light, of course. They could navigate in total darkness. I'd seen them coming out of the restricted areas, black tunnels in the center of the Hive. But Lowforms needed light. That wouldn't be a bad job for Chen. Inside and out, fresh air and protection. I'd still see him sometimes, coming in from the sea if I was a Diver.

The sound of trickling water echoed up the corridors. Down and down we went. Finally we gathered in one of the huge chambers where the underground rivers flowed. There was a great network of water down here, nearly as convoluted as the Master-made hallways above. I had dived through as many as I was allowed, carrying glowstones down into the darkness to search for the little scuttling waterbugs that were another of the Masters' favorite foods. I preferred the open sea, but Divers had to be comfortable anywhere, and I was determined to win.

There was no need of the glowstones here. The walls were covered in a blue slime that glowed brighter than the rocks. Anywhere the deep river flowed down here was lit with that soft blue light. It didn't extend into the water, dark and rushing at our feet.

We each grabbed a small bag of stones for our dive, and another empty bag for collection. Chen was eyeing the dark, rushing water with evident terror.

"Just do what you can," I whispered to him. "I'll try and get you a couple so you don't come in last."

He nodded, hands trembling on his bag of stones.

"If you get too deep, drop the stones."

He nodded again. We would lose points for dropping stones, but it was all too easy to get lost in the warren of water.

He would have to stay very close to this central chamber.

Not me. I was never lost in the rivers. No matter where I was in the water, all I had to do was feel the direction of the current, and I knew where I was. The older Divers said I'd ventured farther out away from the Hive than most of them ever did, popping up into cavern after cavern for air. Some of those hidden caverns were beyond beautiful, with dripping stalactites covered in glittering crystals. Holes in the roofs let sunlight come slanting in, and tiny flying creatures flapped in and out when it was evening. I never got to see the flapping things up close, but wherever they roosted had a horrible, sick smell.

The Master clicked out our instructions. "Waterbugs. Most." This time each of us had a large basket to put our catch into, instead of a circle scraped into sand like on the beach.

I was first into the water, taking a huge breath as I dove. My strategy was to get far away from the other boys as fast as possible. The waterbugs we were collecting would scuttle away into cracks on the river's floor as soon as they saw our lights. The more boys that tried to hunt them, the fewer there would be.

I kicked away upstream, knowing I'd be tired after a long hunt. Easier to swim upstream now while I was fresh and drift back down with a full load.

The stones in my bag lit my way where the river flowed under solid rock. I swam hard through the empty water. Up ahead was a small pool of light, with waving plant fronds anchored to the river's bottom. The plants needed light to grow, and the water was dotted with them. Waterbugs loved them, and for that reason, so did I.

One. Two. Three. Lightning-fast I grabbed them, feeling their hard carapaces wriggling under my hands. Into the bag at my waist.

I rose to the surface, grabbing at the edge of the hole in the cave ceiling where the light shone through. It was just large enough to stick my face up and grab a few long breaths, which I did before diving back down.

Another boy, Miguel, was searching through the fronds I had just hunted, and I swam on, farther upstream. The cave forked up ahead, and I knew anyone following me would turn right. The path down the left corridor was much longer to the next air hole, and no one but me would likely take the chance. I turned left and kicked against the current.

Darkness and water. I knew each turn and counted them off in my head as I swam. *Large boulder on the left. Deep hole on the right. Duck under the low pass. Around where the tunnel caved in last year. Right at the fork.*

Finally I saw the light, impossibly far away. *Kick and glide, pull and stroke.* My lungs burned.

I popped up, gasping for breath. The current wanted to pull me back down the corridor, but I swam around to where a huge vine trailed from one of the holes in the roof down into the water and grabbed onto it, resting for a moment. This chamber was huge, with lots of openings to the sky. The air was full of screeching calls from inside the cave and outside. My sense of direction told me I was nearly halfway to the mountains, far out under the forest surrounding the grassy fields.

It was a great place to hunt for waterbugs. All the sunlight and open air meant tons of plants grew all around the edges and bottom of the river. I dove down, darting in and out of the vegetation, snatching up bugs from every dark crevasse. Soon my bag was bulging with squirming bugs. I put even more in the bag that held the few glowstones I carried. After all my years in the water, I didn't need the light, only the ballast, so there was room for more bugs.

Stuffed to brimming, both bags tickled against my legs.

A large, dark shape shadowed the water beneath me and I pushed myself out of the way as a river beast surfaced next to me. It puffed air out of its hairy face, ignoring me completely. The river beasts were huge, much longer and fatter than a Lowform. They had thick, short hair all over their bodies and soft, furry faces. They were strong swimmers with wide tails that propelled them through the water moving from one patch of vegetation to the next. I was always startled to run into one, but they were no danger to anyone, and often seemed playful when they encountered us.

"No time to play today. I need to win this."

It puffed again and turned a baleful eye on me, whiskers fluttering, before it dove back down to browse on the plants in the bright shallows.

Time to head back.

The current carried me easily, reversing my course. I flowed along in the darkness until I reached the green glow of the entry chamber. Once there, I paused, looking around. A few of the boys were scrambling around the edges, too afraid to leave the safety of the known. They wouldn't collect more than a couple of waterbugs if they were lucky.

I spotted Chen, bobbing at the surface. From below, I tugged on his leg and he descended, cheeks puffed.

From my overstuffed bag, I pulled handfuls of waterbugs, carefully pushing them into Chen's bag before grabbing his hand and pulling him to the surface.

We scrambled out of the water and pulled our bags up to the baskets. Each waterbug had to be smashed on the head with a rock so it wouldn't scuttle out of the basket. It was messy work, but by the time I was done, my basket was full.

"Thanks, Noah. I owe you." Chen smashed the bugs I'd given him with a grin.

We were each only allowed one dive for this challenge, and I was almost the last one back. Once my bugs were dead, I scanned the boys, each standing next to their baskets. Gil was there, with what looked like only three or four bugs. Chen had more, and I grinned at that.

Everyone was back except Miguel. He was a strong swimmer, and my heart beat faster with every minute he didn't return. There were so many dangers in the river. It was easy to get lost in the dark, underwater caves. Some of the passages ended in tunnels too small to swim through. If you swam down one of those and realized there was no way out, you might not have the strength to swim back.

I clicked to the Masters. "Miguel lost. I find."

They clicked negative.

We waited.

I tried again. "Miguel lost. I go."

Negative.

Chen shivered next to me, rubbing his wet arms. "He should be back by now. Maybe he's in one of those caverns you told me about."

"Maybe." I watched the water's surface, flowing by in the dim green light.

I appealed one more time to the Masters. "Miguel good

Diver. Lots of bugs. I find."

They conferred silently for a moment, then clicked. "Yes."

I dove straight in. Miguel had been searching at the fork upstream. He wouldn't have followed me to the left, and if he had, I'd have passed him on the way back. He had to have turned right. There were a lot more air holes on that path, but none led to anything as big as my favorite hunting cavern.

Halfway to the next air hole, I saw him. The light from his glow bag lit his face from below. He bobbed in the middle of the water column, anchored to one of the waving fronds that had become tangled in his carry bag. His eyes were open and sightless.

I pulled at the bag, tearing the fronds until he was free, and grabbing his limp arm. He floated along behind me as I darted down the tunnel. When I reached the cavern, the other boys helped me pull him out of the water. We beat on his chest and pushed water out of his stomach, but his eyes stayed fixed and open and he took no breaths. After a few minutes the Masters clicked at us to stop.

One of them picked Miguel up in its huge claws and carried him up out of the chamber. The rest of us watched in silence.

"Carry food," the other Master clicked, and we all picked up our baskets of bugs.

I won the day's diving with the most bugs in my basket.

We left Miguel's empty basket sitting alone in the dim green cavern.

CHAPTER 5

NOAH

I did not sleep well the night Miguel died. He had been one of our bunkmates since we were taken from the Mothers' Hall over ten years ago. We had trained together, talked late into the night together, laughed at silly things together, and dreamed together of our futures. He never wanted to be anything but a Diver. Didn't aspire to Queen's Service, like I did. Miguel was a friend, and the empty corner where he usually slept echoed every breath I took.

My dinner of green soup and one of the bugs I'd harvested lay solid in my stomach.

We'd had empty corners before. Sometimes boys just disappeared. Men, too. On the rare occasion when someone disobeyed an order from a Master, or strayed into a forbidden area of the Hive, more often than not, they would just disappear. The Hive had no place for anyone that wasn't a perfect part of our shared home. We never mourned those we lost like that. The Masters knew what was best, and how to keep us safe from Lowforms that couldn't follow the rules.

"Hey, Noah, you awake?" Chen whispered from his place on the hard floor next to me.

"Yeah."

"Are you okay?"

I thought about it. I knew he was asking because I had been the one to pull Miguel's lifeless body from the water. It wasn't the first time I had seen a dead body. There had been other Divers over the years that stayed down too long or came up too fast. They gurgled and screamed, doubled over in pain, clawing at the water's surface. If we got to them in time, they usually died some days later. If we didn't, they would sink beneath the waves, and eventually parts of them would wash up on shore, having provided meals for all the things that dwelled in the sea. *We take from the ocean, and it demands payment from us.* We knew the risk.

But this was Miguel. And that was the right word, wasn't it? It WAS Miguel. He was no longer part of our present, or our future. Everything Miguel had been was now in the past. That transition was what ate at me that sleepless night.

"Yeah," I replied to Chen. "I'm okay."

Poor Miguel. He should never have ventured so far from the entry pool. If he hadn't been so determined to do well in the Ranking, he would still be alive tonight.

With the Masters, there was no question of who did what. They were born for their tasks, and each one had the tools from the time they emerged from their pupal stage. Diggers had huge foreclaws for gouging out the deep tunnels that crisscrossed under the Hive. Builders had great, gaping mouths which they filled with dirt and wood from the forest, chewing the mass into a paste which hardened into the towering walls that protected us. Soldiers emerged with wicked sharp pincers on their forelegs, and the paralyzing, venomous tail spikes. Every Master knew what it was from the moment it popped out of its cocoon. Only Lowforms had to struggle so hard to learn our place. Miguel was right to give his all. I just wished I'd taken that tunnel. Maybe I could have found him in time.

In the morning we slurped down our breakfast and assembled in a corridor at the edge of the Lowforms' permitted area

One by one, a Master took us into a room. Those of us left outside timed the one inside by the fading of a glowstone. Each boy got the same amount of time in the room, and when one was finished, the Master would send him away so that he couldn't talk to the rest of us. We had no idea what was in the room. Our numbers dwindled until only a few of us were left in the dimming glow.

The Master clicked at me. "Now. You."

I jumped up and followed it into the corridor. We made several turns, which I noted absently, trotting along behind the Master. This was one of the smaller Master Soldiers, more recently emerged and still in an immature molt. Its carapace would crack as it grew a new one inside, over and over until it achieved its final, massive size. For now, when it stood on its hind legs, its mouth was even with mine.

We arrived at the opening to a room. It was brightly lit with fresh stones, but I couldn't see inside past the Master.

"Go. Build. Fast."

The Master stepped back and I scuttled into the room,

following the direction of its front leg gesture.

Build? Build what? We weren't Builders. The Masters built the Hive. Female Lowforms wove baskets and clothing. What was I supposed to build?

The room's floor was littered with unfamiliar objects. I glanced back at the Master, who stood in the doorway watching me. *Build what?*

I crouched down and examined the nearest piece. It was made of hard, smooth metal, a large round disk with a hole in the center. There were smaller holes around the edges. The same metal edged the huge vats of algae that made up our food, strong and dark, non-reflective. It made a flat sound when I tapped my fingernail against it.

The other objects were even stranger. There was a metal tube, as big as the soft, colorful tubes in the sea that had long, feathery gills to sweep the water but would retract if a Diver swam too close. When I held this heavy thing up in front of me, I could see a faint reflection in it, of my own puzzled face, and the expressionless Master behind me.

Build?

I looked back at the disk. The hole in the center looked about the same size as this tube. I experimented for a moment, pushing the two together, until I was rewarded with a satisfying click. The two pieces were joined into one, a disk with a tube sticking out the top. Had I done it? A glance back to the Master said no.

What else was there?

The next piece was large and flat, covered in some kind of cloth, with a thick weave and dull colors. The bottom of the piece was made of the same smooth metal as the disk, and it had a small hole in the middle. That hole clicked nicely into the tube on the disk. Put together and set upright, it made a small platform, with the woven side up.

There was another large piece, nearly identical to the cloth-covered platform I'd just put together, but longer. It had no hole in it, but on closer examination, I noticed a flat piece of metal sticking out the bottom with four tiny holes. Further searching revealed a pile of tiny metal tubes with spirals etched into their length, and a small, flat line on the wider top.

What were these things? Where had they come from? And how much time did I have left?

The Master in the doorway said nothing.

Three more pieces sat on the floor. Two were the same; cloth-covered and oblong, and one was different, a long metal stick with a hard yellow end that fit perfectly in my hand. The tip of the stick was flat.

Like the ends of the tiny, spiral tubes. Which would maybe fit in the little holes.

I looked all over the platform, searching for a place to put the tubes. On the underside of the platform, little holes matched up perfectly to the other pieces I had. I laid the platform on the side, and held the largest piece up to the holes that fit. The tiny tubes fit into the holes, and when I pushed the stick into the flat groove in the tube, it was obvious that it got tighter when I spun it in one direction.

How much time was left? Had I been in this room forever?

I matched up the other pieces on each side of the platform and attached them the same way. It looked funny like that, so I flipped it back up onto the circular base.

Of course. It was meant for a Lowform to sit on. After

a quick glance at the Master, I tried it out. The strange cloth was surprisingly soft when I sat on it, and my arms rested naturally on the two side pieces. Who had made this amazing thing? Was this the only one? I'd never seen anything like it.

The Master in the doorway clicked at me. "No-build." It meant for me to take it apart.

As I reached for the stick, I thought about the object, taking it apart piece by piece. Had I done it right? Was I the fastest to put it together? Would it be enough? I placed each piece back where I'd found it, setting the room for the next boy. If only I could tell Chen about it . . . give him an idea of what he was supposed to make. But he was smart. Probably smarter than me. He'd figure it out.

I followed the Master away from the chamber, and sat outside in the sun, waiting for the rest of the boys to finish the challenge.

In just a short while, we'd know.

CHAPTER 6

NOAH

Chen didn't figure it out. We whispered about it when he
came outside, waiting for the last boy to finish his time.

"I froze," he said, sitting on the ground on the flat, rocky
patch between the Hive and the beach with his head in his
hands. "I could sort of see what I was supposed to do, but
every time I picked something up, I just kept looking at the
Master in the doorway. I got the tube on the disk, but the
stick-thing just didn't make any sense. It seems so obvious
now."

"It will be all right," I said. "You did well enough at
everything. And you're a great gardener. The Masters know
that. I think you'll get it."

We waited forever, as the afternoon sun fell behind the
massive Hive. A hot wind still blew in from the sea, and
the screeching cries of little insects filled the air. Around us,

Masters and Lowforms scurried, doing their daily tasks. A group of Soldiers exited the Hive, heading out on a patrol. There were two Lowform Runners with them, and they filed along up the beach. I watched them until they were out of sight.

Finally the last boy came up. I could tell from his face that he hadn't figured out how to build the thing. Was I the only one?

Across the rocks I could hear Gil boasting. I wasn't the only one. He built the Lowform seat as well. One other boy, Jerome, seemed to have gotten it most of the way finished. Everyone else had either choked under the pressure, or been totally baffled about how the parts fit together.

Maybe that was it. Maybe I'll get it.

All of the younger boys trooped out and formed a circle around us. I'd done this every year since I was taken out of the nursery, watching the older boys learn their fates. Fifty or sixty kids moved into silent order, with us in the middle. Three of the Masters scuttled out of the Hive and approached our little group, cutting through the circle of younger boys. We all jumped up and stood at attention. The Masters stood with their hind ends toward the sun, and I had to squint against the fiery sky to see them. My eyes burned.

"Rank finished," the center one clicked. "Jobs."

One by one they clicked out our names. Three of the boys ended up as Cleaners. They rushed inside to join the ranks of men who hauled waste from the Hive, both Lowform and Masters', and dragged it out to the sea. It was hard work, but they would grow strong. Two were named as Runners. This was odd, as Gil had beaten both of them in the footrace. Their chests puffed with pride as they strutted into the Hive. Soon they'd leave with Soldiers. If they were lucky, they'd come back with them. If not, they'd give their lives in service to the Hive. Ultimately, we all would.

Three more made Gardener. Chen's face fell that he wasn't among them.

"I thought I'd get it," he whimpered.

I wanted to throw an arm around him, but there were only a few of us left, now, and the Masters were watching.

The Master pointed at Chen, and he snapped to attention.

What would it be? Where would my best friend spend the rest of his life?

"Caretaker."

My throat closed up. Beside me, Chen sobbed a quick cry from deep in his belly.

"No . . . not that. Please . . ." But there was no begging with Masters. Our personal wants were deep beneath them. All served the Hive.

I watched Chen slump toward the entrance. He turned back and took a long, deep breath, eyes wandering across the rocky edge toward the sea. This was his last moment of sunlight. He would be taken to the Mothers' Hall, to live the rest of his days in the dim caverns, surrounded by females and crying babies.

Oh, Chen. I'm so sorry.

My view of him got blurry for a moment and I wiped my eyes on the back of my hand. When I looked back, the entrance was empty. Chen was gone.

Five more of us waited outside.

"Divers," clicked the Master, and my ears perked up. This should be me.

It wasn't.

The two boys named hugged each other and raced for the Hive door. Divers had the best sleeping chambers, and extra shellfish and bug rations. They were made.

The remaining three of us looked at each other. Me. Jerome. And Gil.

My heart pounded in my dry throat.

What was left? Had they forgotten us?

The Master clicked for attention, and pointed at us one, two, three.

We each straightened as its pincer aimed our way.

I stared into the setting sun, with the tall, graceful silhouette of the Master in front of it. I breathed deep, as Chen had done, savoring the clean, salty air in my nose. In moments, my life's fate would be revealed to me.

The Master's mandibles clicked.

"Queen's Service."

I looked at Jerome and Gil, whose faces held the expression I knew I wore as well. *Did it just say what I think it said? Is it real?*

Gil gave a loud whoop and pumped a fist into the air. A whooshing laugh escaped my throat. Jerome just looked dumbfounded. He wasn't a great diver, or a fast runner. He wasn't strong like me. But something must have told the Masters that he was worthy of the highest honor in the Hive. We would pass through the boundary where no other Lowforms were permitted. We would enter the service of the Queen herself. Beyond that, we didn't know. Queen's Servants never returned to the main Hive. They were far above the rest of the Lowforms. Hardly as exalted as a Master, but . . . Queen's Servants.

All around, the younger boys cheered for us.

Now the tears streamed from my eyes, as I joyfully followed the Masters into the Hive.

I had done it. I was entering the Queen's Service. My heart still broke for Chen's dismal fate, but this moment belonged to me. I had barely dreamed it was possible, and yet here I was, descending toward the glorious unknown.

"Can you believe it?" Jerome whispered as we paraded past the other Lowforms waiting in line for their evening meal. "I can't believe it."

Gil answered, "Of course I can. Never had a doubt."

I said nothing, basking in the admiring glances of all the Lowforms we passed. We were better than the Gardeners, with their fungus-stained hands. So much better than the Cleaners, who always smelled sour. Better even than the Divers, who nodded as we filed past.

Noah, Queen's Servant.

I lifted my chin and followed my Masters deep into the Hive, where my Queen waited to command me.

CHAPTER 7

CHEN

I couldn't believe my ears.

Caretaker.

The worst of all possible jobs in the Hive.

I lunged toward my best friend Noah, who was standing there with his mouth open. Giant Digger claws grabbed me from behind and pulled me toward the opening to the Hive. It had always been my home. Noah and I had dreamed about our futures here, how we'd be important men, respected by all the Masters for how hard we worked. He was going to be a Diver, and I was going to be a Gardener. Together, we would provide food for the whole Hive, securing our honor among the Masters and the Lowforms.

Everything crashed down in that instant.

I shook off the Digger that was hauling me toward the Hive, and clicked to it. "I go."

It released me and I turned back to the sunlight one final time. Noah stood there across the sandy plateau, along with Gil and Jerome. The pity on Noah's face made me want to throw up. Beyond them, waves crashed into the shore, throwing white foam up against the rocks around the beach. The air smelled of salt and shellfish, fresh and wild. Sunlight played on the ocean as far as I could see.

Never again.

I took a last, deep breath and turned into the dark doorway for the last time.

The walls closed in around me as I trudged deep into the Hive, the Digger at my back. It had never felt like this before. I'd always welcomed the safety of our thick walls, and the protection of our brave Soldiers. I'd be safe in the Mothers' Hall for the rest of my life. Safe in the dark, underground chamber full of screaming babies. Safe from the fresh air above, from the sunlight, from the water. Safe from everything that made it a life. Forever.

The turnoff to the Mothers' Hall was guarded by two more Diggers. My protectors, now. I hadn't been beyond this tunnel since they brought me out as a little child. I had no memory of my mother or father. Were they still here? Would they know me when I came back? I'd soon find out.

The Diggers let me pass. I entered the dark tunnel.

Along each side, smaller rooms held women with babies. Up ahead, sound echoed out of a larger chamber. I didn't know where to go or what to do, so I just walked ahead. The corridor was dark, lit by the occasional glowstone. Dim light filtered from ahead, and as I passed the side rooms, women came shuffling out. They wore long tunics like me, and had their hair braided into elaborate coils. They were every shade of skin color, just like the Lowform boys I'd grown up with.

At the end of the hallway I entered a large, open room. A few open shafts obviously led to the surface, sunlight beaming in through narrow shafts, making bright points on the smooth, hard floor. Toddlers ran around, and babies cried from every hip.

A man blocked my way.

"You the new one?"

I shrank back from him. He was old, maybe twenty-five. Brown like me, with a single long braid of hair down his back. He looked strong and his eyes held no welcome.

"I'm Chen. Caretaker." I tried to act proud about my Ranking. Taking care of the women and babies was important. Without babies, there would be no Lowform workers. And we did so much around the Hive.

"Chen," the man said. He turned to the women clustering around me. "It's Chen!" he called. "Anybody know Chen?"

A girl a little older than me squealed and ran up to me. She wrapped her arms around me, squishing the baby she carried between us. It cried and I pulled away, staring at the girl.

"Chen!" she cried. "You're my brother!"

I didn't even know the word.

"We had the same mother," she explained. "She was older, and was taken up a few years ago, but she remembered the names of all her children." She beamed at me. "I'm Glenna." She hoisted the baby up to my face. "And this is Lee, who's your nephew."

She ushered me farther into the room. Everyone wanted to be close to me, hands reaching out to touch me. I realized this must be the most exciting thing that ever happened down here . . . when a new boy was sentenced to life in the darkness. Next time someone was Ranked as Caretaker, it would be me pressing forward with the women and babies, wanting to see the new arrival, maybe hear stories of the outside world I was locked away from.

Glenna hugged me again. My sister. Holding my nephew. I still didn't really understand what that meant, but it seemed important to her.

"Come and meet Shari," she said, pulling my hand. "She's your sister, too."

A very pregnant woman waddled over and threw her arms around me in a sweaty hug. I tried not to squirm, but I'd lived my whole memory with other boys my age. We weren't huggers. The woman's belly pressed into mine and the horror on my face must have shown.

"Chen," Shari said, hand on her stomach. "I'm so glad you're here. We needed a male with your bloodline." She glanced at the man who had met me at the entrance. "Need to keep track."

There were a few other men around, and an older boy I remembered from a few Rankings back.

They looked happy.

I'd expected a miserable bunch, withering away in darkness. But their faces shone with joy and welcome.

Shari and Glenna ushered me to a seat on the ground near one of the sun rays. The rest of the people sat around in a circle. Older toddlers ran around the group, playing with the hard-shelled remains of the waterbugs that must have been their breakfast. Maybe the ones Noah had helped me collect.

I thought about him, outside awaiting his fate. He'd

make Diver for sure. My heart filled with pride for him. My best friend, a Diver. I would think of him with every shellfish I ever ate.

"Oh, Chen," Glenna said. "We're so happy you're here. There's so much we need to tell you."

I looked at my sister. The sunlight cast long shadows under her eyes. In her arms, the baby slept, tiny hands gripping one of the skinny braids that hung from Glenna's head.

"I'm happy to be here," I lied. "Here with my nephew." I thought that was the right word.

She beamed down at the baby for a moment, before her eyes turned serious and she met my gaze.

"Down here, we remember," she said. "Chen, what we're going to tell you won't be easy to hear. But it's the truth, and it comes straight from the stars."

Her eyes held mine. "Everything you've been told your whole life has been a lie."

CHAPTER 8

NOAH

Down and down we walked. A basket of glowstones had been thoughtfully set at the edge of the boundary, and when the Masters indicated one of us was to carry it, I jumped fastest and grabbed it. The tunnels grew darker, and we followed the clicking sound of the Masters' hard feet on the floor. The glowbasket only lit a few paces in front of us, and we huddled together in its light. Masters had no need of it, and skittered ahead of us.

The quiet pressed in on my ears. No hallways bisected ours, and no chambers branched off. There was only this long, twisting corridor, ever downward into the forbidden heart of the Hive.

Up ahead, I could feel the corridor widen. The light of the glowbasket reflected off the walls around us, but the Masters left us behind and entered into a chamber that emitted its own glow from the damp blue slime. One of them turned back to us and clicked in its elegant language.

"Prepare for Queen."

I had no idea what it meant. The Masters scuttled around us, pulling at our tunics and adjusting our loose pants. The tunics were long and loose, worn with a sash around the waist, which the Masters bit straight through and pulled away, dropping them into a pile of cloth at the edge of the room. They touched us all over with their soft feelers, and I held in a sneeze when the feeler tickled my nose.

Finally it was time.

"Come. Silent."

The Hive's highest honor was upon us. I doubted any of us could make a sound even if we wanted to.

They led us across the room to a round, open doorway. I left the glowbasket where it sat, because the room beyond the doorway emitted enough light that I wouldn't need it. The sound of trickling water reached my ears from somewhere beyond, and the air was damp and still.

The Masters entered the room before us and we filed in behind. They blocked our view, pressing us back into the walls.

When they moved, my eyes filled with a glory I couldn't imagine.

The Queen.

She took up almost the entire chamber. Her body was shaped like the Master Soldiers around her, which I had always thought were enormous but now were dwarfed by her magnificence. She had a tiny head at the top of her thorax, which lacked the hard armor of the smaller Masters around her. She sat rocked back on a wide rear end that disappeared behind her so that all eight of her legs waved toward us. Her thorax was almost white in the dim glow.

One by one the three Masters approached her. They bowed their heads before the soft, pale thorax, honoring the Queen. The first stepped forward, and she lowered her head. The Soldier rubbed its head against the top of the Queen's. She wrapped four of her legs around the Soldier's body, two Masters wrapped together. When the Soldier stepped back, a white, waxy sheen of oil covered its head, and it sagged for a moment, forelegs limp in awe. The Queen clicked at it and it backed up, allowing the next to receive her moist blessing.

I ached to follow them. I could almost feel how it would be to rub my own head into hers. She would fold her legs around me as she did them, and I would belong to her forever. Was this the secret? Was I worthy of such glory?

The smallest Master I had ever seen scuttled around the edge of the chamber. He crawled right over the Queen's back without a glance at us. *The King. Father of the whole Hive.* His head only came up to my waist, but I wanted to bow before him.

The Queen clicked at the Masters, and they turned to where we huddled against the wall, stupefied in awe in the presence of the enormous, hulking Queen. One Master stood in front of each of us.

There was no signal that I could hear. No click from Queen or Master.

In an instant, the Masters swung their tails around, digging their stingers into us.

My breath caught in my throat. It broke the spell of the Queen, and I whipped my head around to see Gil and Jerome on either side of me mirroring my posture, hands clutching at the sides of their bellies where the sting had caught them.

I knew what came next. The Masters used those stings to protect us from lesser insects that would steal our food and invade our Hive. My mind got fuzzy as my body weakened. I couldn't feel my hands or feet. I flopped to the floor, my head banging against Jerome's knee. I tried to roll over, to cry out a question, but all I could do was flail on the floor. Numbness crept up my arms and legs until my twitching stopped. My heart pounded, and my breathing was soft and slow. My eyes darted around the room, the only part of me I could move.

Was this some ritual? Some final test?

The Masters dragged Jerome away from where I lay, and my head, which had been propped on his knee, banged into the ground. It didn't hurt, but I couldn't turn my neck to follow where they took him. I stared at the ceiling, which faded from the bright blue of the slimy walls into a black, featureless cave overhead, and listened to the sounds around me. There was a soft, squishy sound, then the grating of a boy being dragged away.

They came for Gil.

My mind was still fuzzy, drifting in and out of focus. It seemed like no time at all before they came for me.

I couldn't feel them grab my shoulders, or the rough sliding of my butt on the floor as they dragged me around behind the Queen. What I had seen as her backside turned out to be the start of a huge, fat tail. It reared up around her, and as the tip of it descended toward me, I had a moment to bask in her glory once more. She was going to touch me with her tail. Me. Noah. The Queen was going to touch my skin.

They laid me down and her tail approached me. The tip was round and wet, quivering in the blue light. The Masters pulled my tunic up to my neck.

Her tail dropped beyond my vision. I couldn't feel her touching me. But out of the extreme lower corners of my eyes, I could see it. The sight should have filled me with rapture as her tail touched my skin. Instead I was filled with horror at the grotesque sight.

Eggs. Each time her tail contacted my skin, it squeezed out a glistening, translucent egg the size of my fist. Along with each one came a sticky white goo that cemented the eggs onto my skin. One by one she deposited them onto me, covering my exposed belly with soft round eggs.

It lasted forever. The squishing sound of each deposit screamed betrayal into my ears. But this was my Queen. This was the highest honor in the Hive. I'd worked all my life to get here, and the joy I should have felt at her attention warred with the numb fear in my paralyzed body.

Finally it was finished. The Masters dragged me away behind her, out another open doorway.

If I could have screamed, the corridors would have echoed with sound. But all I could hear was the steady trickle of water, and the gritty noise of my body as they dragged me away from the majesty of our enormous Queen.

CHAPTER 9

NOAH

The Master dragged me out through the open archway behind the Queen. I couldn't move a muscle, just flop along in numb paralysis. My mind whirled. She had touched me. Our majestic Queen had touched me. My stomach was covered in her eggs. But the glory of the moment gave way to my dawning horror as the Master dragged me farther from her exquisite presence.

The caverns on this level were all covered in the glowing slime. Shallow pools of standing water flanked each side of the path I slid across. Although I couldn't turn my head, I could see to each side.

In each of the pools lay shapeless forms, ringing the edges and extending into the water. In that first chamber, I couldn't tell anything more than that.

The next chamber held more of the pools. The forms

that ringed the edges were more recognizable here. Six or eight to a pool, the great gray water beasts were positioned with their heads out of the water and what remained of their bodies submerged. The beasts were all dead, shriveled husks, thin and hollow.

In the next chamber, the truth became so obvious that even in my confused state I could hardly miss it. The water beasts were still alive. So were the boys.

Two boys that had disappeared over a week ago lay alongside the beasts, their heads on the edge and bodies in the water. Their chests were sunken, cheeks sagging under dull skin. Only their slow breathing and the darting of their wide eyes hinted that they still lived. An older woman lay next to them in the same state.

Their bellies were squirming masses of larvae. Beast and Lowform alike were covered in giant larvae, each as thick as my thigh and as long as my forearm. Shiny and pale, their bodies waved in the shallow water, heads buried in the living flesh of their hosts. And beside them all lay the Feral from the beach, the pale thing that had burst from the trees and run straight for me. He had been stripped of his clothing, the eggs on his belly large and glistening.

The Master dragged me into the next room. Four of the water beasts were already positioned around the shallow pool, submerging the eggs cemented into their gray skin in the warm water. Gil and Jerome had been laid next to them, faces out and bodies in. Their chests rose and fell slowly, making ripples in the dirty water. Their bellies were covered in eggs, tunics pulled up around their necks. The Master laid me next to Jerome.

I struggled to move, but my arms and legs felt as if they

were no longer attached to my head. My eyes moved a bit, but I couldn't turn my head to meet the gaze of the boys on each side of me. It was just as well. What could our panicked eyes have shared?

There was no illusion in my mind. This was how I would die. Emotions warred inside my still body as I lay there in the pool, listening to the quiet breaths of the water beasts, my friends, and myself. Was there any higher honor than to die for the Queen? To give my body to nourish new Masters? In a tiny way, I would be part of those Masters who were born of my flesh. Though I would die, I might live in them.

Idiot. You're nothing to them. You're no better than a stupid water beast. Worse, actually. You walked willingly to your own death.

The thought seemed to come from some other Noah. Never in my fifteen years could I have imagined such treacherous ideas.

But it's true. You're no different than a shellfish. They harvest you and still you thank them for it.

I wanted to scream, but no sound came from my throat.

The glowing blue walls faded to black overhead in the quiet cavern.

M̲y finger twitched. It made a little splashing sound in the water.

It's wearing off. Maybe you can escape.

I concentrated, willing the finger to twitch again.

The finger was stubborn, but my right toe responded.

Yes! That's it. Move the foot. Stand up. Run.

I was almost able to wiggle my whole right foot when my vision darkened as a Master loomed over me. Its tail made a whooshing noise as it swung around to sting me, but I felt nothing.

My foot went still.

The betrayal was agony.

I trusted them. Worshiped them. Our magnificent Masters, who cared for us and protected us . . . how could they use me like this?

Because it's what you were born for. They are great, and you are small. Be glad you can serve in this way.

The unuttered scream rose in my throat. We breathed in darkness.

CHAPTER 10

NOAH

I couldn't count how many times the cycle repeated. A tiny part of me would tingle, angry shards poking from the inside of my skin. I would struggle to move, to regain control of my limbs. The Masters would return and sting me back into paralysis. It could have been hours, days, or weeks. I was dimly aware of Jerome and Gil on each side of me. Were the same thoughts of betrayal and rage pounding in their minds? Did they remain loyal to the Queen? With each passing moment, the anguish grew. I hated her. I hated them. The Queen I had so revered was nothing more than a pale, fat, egg-spewing monster, crouching in darkness in a room she had grown to fill. If I could have moved, I'd have run in to her chamber and ripped her head from her thorax. I imagined how it would taste as I lay there. My mandibles would crush her old carapace, and the juice from her body would run down my armor.

You don't have mandibles. You're a Lowform.

But the image wouldn't leave my brain.

The eggs hatched.

I couldn't feel the larvae that buried their heads into the skin of my belly. There was no pain as they started to suck the life from my body. My rage grew with each wave of their slimy tails, splashing in the water.

My left index finger twitched. My left toe. The angry shard pain needled into my right calf, cramping the muscle. Where the larvae burrowed into my skin, it started to sting, the numbness of the venom wearing off. My vision darkened with the shadow of a Master. Three of them crowded around us and I waited for the sting that would take the pain away. *Just a few more. Soon they'll have taken all I have to give, and this final nightmare will end.*

The Masters didn't sting us.

They lifted us out of the water in turns, running their feelers over the larvae on our bellies. The clicking they made was so fast I couldn't understand them. My back burned as they dragged me out of the water, pulling my wet tunic down to cover the larvae.

My arm twitched, and my head lolled to the side as a Master Digger picked me up in its strong forelimbs. Leaving the water beasts in the pools, they carried me, Gil, and Jerome out of the chamber and into the dark corridor beyond.

My body was wracked with pain. Every inch of my skin screamed with fire as the Masters' paralyzing venom wore off. Great spasms lurched through me, and the Master carrying me tightened its grip. I had no control over my arms and legs, flailing them around like a waterbug held in the air.

They carried us through passages I had never entered, beyond the boundary where Lowforms were allowed. In a dark hallway, they paused. Noise echoed down the cavern, crashes and bangs, and the harsh screams of Lowforms. In a moment, another Master appeared. It did not click to the ones that carried us, but they followed it up and up.

Light brightened the caverns, and the air smelled fresher. I struggled against the Master that carried me, and it clicked at me to be silent. We entered a hall I recognized, the one that led to the chamber where our huge vats of green slime sat in the sunny chamber that faced the sky. The Masters carried us into that huge room. The holes that led to the sky were covered in cloth now, as they always were during the pollen storm. The chamber was dim. No one stirred, Lowform or Master. Where had everyone gone?

The Masters clicked. "Wait. Still. Silent."

They dumped us on the floor and scuttled away.

"Noah?"

Jerome's voice sounded like rocks rubbing together.

"I'm here," I said, sounding just the same.

"What . . . what's going on?"

I shoved my elbows up under my back, raising up. All three of us were hidden behind the slime vat. Jerome and Gil were still lying flat, but both were moving their arms and legs, flexing their fingers. The moving bulges under their tunics looked the same as mine.

Larvae. They were still eating us alive.

"We have to get these things off us," I grunted. "They're sucking us dead."

I struggled to push myself up against the outer wall of the chamber, shoving my feet into the hard ground. The solid wall tore at my back, but I pushed with my legs, arms splayed against the flat wall. When my fingers found purchase in one of the holes that let sunlight in, I grasped it and hauled myself up. My head felt heavy and soggy, like I'd just come up from too deep a dive. I leaned against the wall and pulled up my sopping wet tunic.

Underneath, the larvae squirmed on my belly. My hands still felt like they belonged to someone else as I grasped one of the larvae and pulled. The shock of pain sent me sliding back against the wall.

They're sucked on to you. Pry them off like a shellfish.

I stuck a finger under the rim of one of the larva's mouth where it joined my skin. With a wet, popping sound, the seal broke. It flailed around in my hand. The sticky white goo that had cemented the eggs to my belly was still smeared all over me and I couldn't drop the writhing maggot. I tried to wipe it on the side of the slime vat but my hand stuck.

Finally I plunged my hand into the slime. The sticky goo let go and the larva dropped away into the murky depth.

One by one I pulled the larvae off, washing them away into the giant vat. The last one held tighter than the rest, and was bigger. It sucked on to my hand as I pulled it free of my belly, and I had to peel it off under the slime. When I was free of the last larva, I looked down at my belly. The skin oozed blood from dozens of perfect rings where the larvae had attached to me. I pulled my tunic back down and turned to help Jerome and Gil, who were just struggling to their feet.

"Pull them off," I said. "They're really sticky. You have to wash them off in the slime or they just stay glued on to you."

A harsh clicking cut me off. The three Masters surrounded us and grabbed us, pinning our arms to our sides and lifting us like we were nothing.

You are. To them, you are nothing.

They each waved their feelers over my tunic and clicked fast.

"Silent. Leave."

I had no idea what they were talking about. I wanted to scream, but what would I say? The Hive was full of Masters. All the Lowforms together weren't a quarter of their number, and four Lowforms would barely match the strength of one. Who would I cry out to?

They carried us out of the food chamber and down the hallway toward a small, side entrance to the Hive. In the doorway, they paused. Outside, the pollen storm raged. The air was full of tiny red dust particles that covered everything. Pollen storms lasted two days each month, when the moons aligned. Every forty-three days it happened, and the Lowforms including myself would have to venture out of the Hive without the protection of our Masters. The Masters hated the pollen. They always stayed safe behind our mud walls, or deep in the tunnels below until the smaller insects cleared the pollen from the hard ground. Would they carry us outside now?

They dropped us in the doorway and held us by the shoulders. Smaller shadows filled the entrance. They smelled unfamiliar, but their shapes were like ours.

Ferals.

Right here in our Hive.

The Masters held us and the Ferals grabbed our hands, winding woven rope around our wrists, binding us tight. They nodded to the Masters, who shoved us out into the storm, tethered to the Ferals. Gil, Jerome, and I were pulled from the Hive, stumbling along behind the Ferals that clutched our binding ropes.

"No!" I shouted into the hot, red wind. But no Master came to save me.

The Ferals tugged our ropes, and we ran across the open field in the haze of the storm.

CHAPTER 11

NOAH

We ran straight down into the Forbidden Zone. I slammed on the brakes as soon as I realized where the Ferals were taking us, but they tugged on my rope, pulling me over the edge. I could barely see the hulking shapes, squinting in the red wind. My eyes streamed with tears and my nose ran.

"We can't . . ." I began, but the Feral holding my rope jerked my arms and I had no choice but to follow.

The shapes were so much bigger up close. They towered over my head, not as tall as the Hive, but longer. Some were bigger than others, and as we passed into their shadows, I realized they were made of the same metal as my prybar, and the odd little tubes I'd used to build the strange seat during the Ranking. A million years ago, or a few days? I wasn't sure. Creeping plants covered most of the surfaces, and some had great openings in their sides, mouths yawning to darkness. Every shape was different, and most appeared severely damaged, caved in and smashed. The ground around was pockmarked from what must have been a huge fall of the rocks that sometimes rained from the sky.

We jogged past the shapes and climbed the hill on the other side. Red pollen filled my nostrils and burned my eyes. My strength was flagging, and I slipped, dropping to my knees. The Feral pulled me up by the rope.

"I know you're tired," it said. "But we have to get clear before the pollen ends."

I goggled at it. Ferals could talk? I remembered the one from the beach. How long ago was it? Felt like years. It had tried to talk as the Soldier's venom flooded its body. Now this Feral spoke the Lowform language.

"You can—" I began, but it pulled at my arms.

"Save your breath. We'll stop for a break once we're into the mountains."

My mind whirled as I followed. The Lowform was male, I could tell that now. He was a lot older than me. All four of the Lowforms that were pulling us along were older males. Could they all talk? I glanced over to Gil and Jerome, but they were plodding along, eyes on the ground. They looked even worse than I felt.

In the low, rocky hills, we paused. The Ferals took out water skins and poured them over the fronts of our tunics before giving us drinks. I realized their clothing was not like ours, but fit much closer around their waists and legs. They wore some kind of thick, stitched hides on their feet.

"You can talk?" I asked the one that held my rope.

He rolled his eyes. "Of course we can talk. What kind of nonsense do those monsters feed you there?"

I shook my head. "Ferals are stupid, like waterbugs. They look like us, but they're not like us. Not worthy of the Hive." The treacherous part of me snickered. *Not worthy to get sucked dry by a bunch of maggots?*

The Feral spat on the ground. "Worthy of the Hive. Listen to you. Brainwashed from the minute you're born." He sighed. "Look, kid. I know this has to seem crazy right now. And I wish there was time to explain everything. But right now you just have to trust us. We're saving your lives." He glanced into the mountain pass where we were headed. "All of our lives."

They fed us some unfamiliar food, soft and chewy, and mostly devoid of flavor. After another quick drink of water, they helped us to our feet and led us farther into the mountains.

We spent the night in a cave on the mountain, shivering on the wet, cold ground. The Ferals kept us bound and tied us to their own waists. They sat us on opposite sides of the cave so we had no chance to untie each other. Jerome looked pale, and two of the Ferals crowded around him. I could hear them whispering, and I had a million questions, but was too exhausted to ask them. I passed out on the ground and woke stiff and sore.

I looked around, blinking in the glow of pre-dawn. The Feral I was tied to grunted and rolled over. I sat up quietly. Gil was still asleep on one side of the cave, and Jerome on the other.

"Gil," I whispered, eyeing the sleeping Ferals. "Gil, wake

up. We need to get out of here."

He twitched in his sleep but did not wake.

"Jerome," I said, looking over to where he slept. He didn't even twitch.

My whispers woke the Feral, who woke the rest of them. He was checking my bindings when a voice across the cave stopped us both cold.

"He's dead."

My head jerked up. One of the Ferals was standing over Jerome. As the dawn light spread into the cave, I could see that he was right. Jerome was still and hollow.

The Feral swore, using a word I'd never heard before.

"Blast it," one of the others said. "But he doesn't have her. I hate to leave them here to die, but we need to get moving."

They pulled out more of the tasteless, chewy food, shoving it into my mouth when I tried to resist.

"I'm sorry about your friend," one of them said to me, "but we have to get out of here. You have to eat or you're going to die, too. It's not that far. Come on, buddy. You can do this."

Hunger won, and I chewed some of the food. They helped me to my feet and we emerged into the dawn, leaving Jerome's body in the empty cave.

By the time we crossed the pass and headed down the other side, the pollen storm was waning. I could see down the valley to another Hive in the distance. This one was nowhere near as large as ours.

Ours? Is it still yours? Was it ever yours at all?

Part of the south wall had collapsed, exposing the inner chambers to the harsh sunlight.

Ferals poured out of the entrance as we approached. A couple of Masters joined them, Builders and Diggers, mostly, hanging back in the shadow of the doorway.

"You did it," one of the Ferals said. "You actually got them out. I can't believe it."

This Feral was smaller than me, female, with long brown hair and brown eyes. She was dressed like the others and eyed my wet tunic. "Did you get her?"

The Feral that held my leash nodded. "The 'Mites said so. She's on this one." He nodded at me and I stared blankly at him.

Another Feral emerged from the Hive. This one was older than any Lowform I'd ever seen. His hair and beard were gray, and wrinkles lined his eyes. He opened spindly hands to indicate the small Hive behind him.

"Welcome, friends," he said. "Welcome to freedom."

CHAPTER 12

NOAH

In the clicking language we shared with the Masters, there was no word for "Welcome." Instead, as Gil and I filed past the waiting Ferals and Masters at the new Hive, the closest Digger clicked out, "Eat here." It was as close as they got.

The feral humans took us inside the Hive, into the large, central chamber dotted with holes to let in the light and air. The few Masters crowded around us, waving their feelers at us. I counted around forty of the Ferals, mostly males. There were a couple of females with babies, and a few small children, and I stared at them. Why were they running free with the worker males? And where were the rest of the Masters that protected this Hive?

Gil looked as mystified as I felt. The Ferals sat us down in front of the old male, untying the ropes that held us. I rubbed my arms where the ropes had cut into my skin, working the circulation back. They handed me water, which I slurped greedily, and more of the tasteless food.

"I'm sorry, boys, but we have to keep you confined for a while," the male said. "We've rescued people before, and it takes a long time before whatever brainwashing those bugs do to you wears off."

A Feral female spoke up. "It's some kind of pheromone thing. Earth bugs used them to communicate, and to bond members of a Hive together. I'm sure whatever it is has some kind of effect on humans."

So many words I didn't recognize. Earth? Humans? I looked at Gil, who shrugged, chewing his bland meal.

The male looked at the other Ferals that had brought us here. "Where's Paul?"

A shake of the head from one of our captors. "He was scouting right before the pollen storm. Watching these boys." He glared at me and Gil. "Got too close and the 'Mites got him."

I remembered his eyes as they dragged him across the beach. I remembered his face as he lay in a pool of dark water, belly covered in eggs.

The old male's eyes dropped, his posture sagging. "Paul was a good man. A very good man. Find your star, Paul." He paused and ran a hand over his face. "But we all knew the risks." He turned to me. "It will be worth it as long as we have her. It's this one, right?"

One of my captors nodded. "That's what the bug said. There were three boys, but we lost one on the way."

The old one's shoulders slumped even further and he looked at me and Gil. "I'm so sorry. We weren't fast enough. What was his name?"

"Jerome," I answered. "His name was Jerome."

The old one looked up toward the ceiling. "Find your star, Jerome." He sighed and rubbed his eyes. "All right. Let's get them down to the pool." He turned to one of the Masters. "Are we ready down there?"

A click from the Master Digger. It rushed up behind me and grabbed my arms, lifting me up. I struggled and screamed as it carried me away from the bright chamber, down into the depths of the Hive. Scuttling noises behind me indicated that Gil had been similarly abducted.

Even as I fought, I was aware of my surroundings. The corridors were dirty, dry and empty. Despite the obvious inhabitants above, the Hive felt dead. It smelled dead. I gave up struggling as the last of my strength left me lolling in the arms of the Master. Down and down it carried me. Footsteps of the Ferals echoed behind us.

We passed through dry, crumbling chambers until we reached one that made my blood chill. Shallow pools were filled with water. Three of the gray water beasts lay still on the edges.

Oh, no. Not again.

The Master set me down and I waited for the sting, squinting my eyes against the expected pain.

The old male Feral approached me and reached for my tunic. "I'm Mo, by the way. Mo Ciel. What's your name, son?"

"Noah," I replied, backing away from him. Could I run? Where? The Masters blocked both doorways to this dank chamber.

He nodded. "Well Noah, let's have a look at her." He gestured to the water beasts in the pool. "They're ready."

My back reached the wall and Ferals grabbed my arms from each side.

"Let's get those nasty things off you . . ." The old male's voice trailed off as he lifted my tunic. Underneath, red welts dotted my belly in perfect circles. His eyes burned into mine. "Where is she? What have you done with her?"

I sputtered.

He reached for Gil's tunic, lifting it to reveal the larvae on his skin.

"Get these off and onto the seals. Hurry up before they suck them dry."

Ferals used their fingers as I had done, unsticking the sucking mouths of the larvae from Gil. They carried the larvae over to the still water beasts and set them on the gray skin. Each larva sucked onto one of the beasts in the water.

I stared until all the larvae had been removed from Gil's stomach. The Masters crowded around the water beasts, caressing the larvae with their soft feelers. They looked up and clicked a word.

"No."

They approached me and Mo pulled up my tunic again. The Masters' feelers tickled the red welts, probing all around until they settled on the largest red ring, the one in the center.

"Here."

The word was clicked with great sadness, and the Ferals looked at each other.

Mo lowered my tunic. "What have you done with her?"

I shook my head. It was all too much for me.

"What have you done?" he repeated. "Where are the larvae that left these wounds?"

"I pulled them off," I stammered. "Back at the Hive.

Washed them off." My teeth were starting to chatter.

Gil slumped to the floor and the Ferals caught him. The old one called Mo sighed. "We've failed. It's all for nothing."

The young female that had met us outside snorted. "It was a crazy idea. Would never have worked anyway."

"It could have," Mo said. "We've shown we can work together." He nodded at the Masters that still hovered around me.

The female shook her head. "They're outcasts. Nobodies, like us. Look, Dad, we'll be okay. We'll just have to find another way." She turned toward Gil, who leaned against the males holding him up. "Right now we need to get some food in these slaves."

Mo turned away from me, shoulders sagging. "You're right, Kinni. Let's get these boys upstairs. They don't need to see this anymore." He swung an arm around the female's shoulder—his offspring? "But you're wrong about them." He turned back toward me and Gil.

"They're not slaves anymore."

CHAPTER 13

NOAH

The days of hosting larvae, the flight through the mountains, and the shocks of today were taking their toll. I followed the Ferals and Masters up the corridors back to the main hall where they all seemed to congregate. They took my wet clothing and dressed me in close-fitting garments like theirs, binding my feet in hides. They fed and watered me, and sat me next to Gil, whose eyelids were drooping.

"I know you boys are tired," Mo said, "but it's important you know some things. This is your home now." He looked around the hall. "Temporarily, anyway. We move a lot, but . . ." He shook his head and started over. "There are things you need to know. Things you were never told. I know you won't believe me tonight, but I swear to you that every word I'm going to tell you is the absolute truth. So just listen now, and in the morning, we'll figure out what we're going to do from here."

Everyone else, Ferals and Masters alike, settled in. Mo faced us all.

"Let's start off with the simplest thing of all. There's no such thing as 'Lowform.' That's not a word we use here." He stared at me and Gil. "You're humans, just like us. And the bugs you call your masters are an alien species that have kept you as slaves for enough generations now that you don't even know the difference."

I didn't know what "slaves" meant. Mo told the story, and I learned.

"Our ancestors came from another star."

My eyes opened wide, and I glanced up toward the ceiling. It was still far too bright for stars to be visible through the little holes. But stars were just tiny lights in the sky, glowstones that kept the night awake. That's what I'd always been told.

I was told wrong.

"Our home planet was doomed, just a few years from total destruction. They picked a bunch of people and sent them off looking for new planets to live on. This was two hundred years ago. My parents were on the ship when she came into orbit, and everyone left the Beta on transports that brought everything they'd need down to the surface."

As he told the story, my exhaustion fell away. So much about it was foreign to me. Everything I'd ever been taught warred with the tale. But it unfolded in my mind, and the betrayal I'd first felt when the Hive Queen laid her eggs on my belly roared back with a bitter taste in the back of my throat.

They landed in the middle of a pollen storm. They circled

the ships in a grassy valley between the mountains and the sea, where clean water flowed down the hills. They couldn't see far in the pollen, but for two days, nothing threatened them.

The night the pollen stopped, the 'Mites attacked.

They swarmed out of the Hive, silent and deadly in the darkness. In a coordinated effort, they attacked the intruders, stinging the sentries and guards before an alarm could be raised. The huge bugs were everywhere. A few people managed to flee into the mountains, but most were dragged into the Hive. Those who escaped tried to return to the transports, but the insects kept watch, and when the people approached, they stung them and carried them away.

They were a true hive mind, singular in purpose, and far from stupid. A few of the humans managed to get into one of their ships and retrieve some weapons. The bugs learned about guns and tanks. Those humans fell to the sheer numbers of the Hive, and as soon as they were dead, the bugs set about dismantling the ships and everything in them. They had learned that humans with their possessions were dangerous. Everything was destroyed and left to rot in the field. The bugs took the big vats of blue-green algae that had sustained the humans on their space voyage, and brought that food into the Hive to feed their new captives.

The story got fuzzy from there.

No one ever learned how the insects figured out a way to control the humans they took. They probably killed most of the adults right away. Probably ate them. I had never realized what likely happened to all the people that disappeared from the Hive in my childhood. But the Masters weren't wasteful.

They learned that humans could swim and dive for food.

They trained the young ones to serve them. Conditioned them from birth to be obedient. Put them to work. Separated the breeding females and babies and took the children from their mothers as toddlers, so they could never learn the truth of who they really were.

I sat there listening to the story of my people, head exploding with concepts I'd never imagined. How was it possible that everything I'd known my whole life was a lie? But as the fog lifted from my eyes, I saw it all, and the shame of ignorance bowed my head.

"They've been breeding you for generations," he said, looking sadly at Gil and me. "They do that thing where they make you compete . . . running and diving. They keep the passive ones, the slow ones, for breeding. They work the ones in the middle until they die. The smartest ones, the ones that might someday figure out the truth and rise up against them . . ." He shrugged. "Well, you're a lot easier to catch than the seals the Queen used to lay her eggs in. You just walk right up and lay down for it. Such an honor."

My face burned. He was right. We did exactly that. And we were obscenely grateful for the chance.

I rubbed the spot on my belly where the largest ring burned. *And was that so bad?*

"There's something in the pheromones the Queen makes. She's got some kind of gland in her head. Rubs it on all the bugs in the Hive, and it bonds them together. Humans don't get it, but it's really powerful. You want it. Crave it. It lets them control you." Mo smiled at us. "That wears off after you've been away for a while." He glanced at the Masters in the room. "Well, sort of. It does for us. Not for them. Once a bug is cast out, they never stop needing a Queen."

Kinni, the young female who was Mo's daughter, spoke up from behind me. "That's what we were counting on. And this idiot ruined it all."

"He didn't know," Mo said, looking at me kindly. "Nobody told him. He shouldn't have been left alone, but what's done is done and we'll have to find another way." He turned back to everyone else. "The human slaves have made that Hive much too powerful. Because of all the extra food and free labor, the Queen of that Hive was able to wage war on all the other Hives around. This one was destroyed early on." He waved a hand at the walls around us. "Hers is the only living Hive for miles around, which would be all right, except for us. She sends her soldiers out to hunt us, and they're good at it. For seventy years our people have been on the run. There's no place safe on this planet. We've lived all over. And the truth is that we don't have enough people to keep going. Not enough women. Not enough babies."

Everyone in the room nodded. I looked around. He was right. The room had a lot more men than women, and hardly any babies.

"We need the women and children the Queen has captive if we're going to survive. And it's long past time for the Queen to die."

My stomach churned at the thought, but I wasn't sure if it was horror or eagerness.

"She's lived far too long," Mo continued. "What's supposed to happen with these bugs is, when the Queen gets old, she lays a new Queen egg. When it hatches and grows up, the new Queen kills the old one. It's a normal thing, keeps the Hive healthy. But this Queen won't let that happen. Whenever she smells a new Queen larva, she kills it right away. Been doing it for years, and it's taking a toll on the Hive. They're getting weaker. Some of the 'Mites there are feeling it. They know it's time for a new Queen. So when we managed to team up with a couple of 'Mites that were cast out of the Hive, we came up with our plan."

The Masters in the back clicked assent.

Not Masters. Bugs. *'Mites, whatever that means.* Insects. That would take some unlearning.

"We have some bugs on the inside. The ones that rescued you and got you out. They waited until they were sure that one of you had the Queen larva, and took you away before the soldiers could come and kill her. They were supposed to get you out and send you here. We had the seals all ready to receive her. We thought that if we raised her ourselves, we could have our own Queen. One that wouldn't be hostile to us. And these 'Mites"—he gestured to the Masters in the room—"assured us that once we had a new Queen, other outcasts from all over would start arriving. We could raise our own army. Take over the big Hive, rescue our people, and . . . live."

I rubbed my belly. Suddenly everything made sense. The biggest larva, the one in the middle. She was a queen. The Queen that would save us all.

And I had thrown her away.

I slept fitfully that night, spinning around on the pile of seal hides they gave me to sleep on. My head was hot, and the ring on my belly ached.

Images of friends I'd lost kept ghosting through my

head. Jerome, eaten alive by larva, just another disposable body to the insects that used us and threw us away. Countless Runners, sent out with Soldiers, never to return. Did the Soldiers even try to save them when danger threatened? Why would they? We were lining up, competing to take their place.

Miguel, drowned in the darkness of the underground river. All he ever wanted to do was be a Diver, collecting food for a Hive that would have left his body to wash away in the current. And the insects hadn't even noticed he was missing.

Humans were nothing to them. Just a resource, like the wood they chewed to build the towering walls that kept us prisoners. And we made it so easy. We were the most eager, happy prisoners, literally dying for the chance to serve our Masters.

I dreamed the faces of the dead, sacrificed to a Hive that had grown powerful on our willing labor.

When I woke up, I was assailed by the smell of the place. Old and gray, the dead Hive smelled of decay and despair.

I rubbed my hand over my belly and sniffed my fingers. Blue.

The welt left by the larval Queen's mouth smelled blue.

I had no other words for the scent. It was vibrant like the late afternoon sky. Blue and beautiful. My Queen. My own Blue Queen.

But she was gone. In my confusion back at the Hive, I had pulled her from my skin, severing our bond forever.

She would have killed you. Sucked you dry.

I knew it was true. I also knew that something inside me had changed. She was mine and I was hers, and without her I would never be whole again.

I plodded outside in the early morning. One of the outcast Masters was there, a Digger with a huge scar on its left front leg, watching me. This was the Master that carried me last night. *Not Masters. 'Mites.* It scuttled over and nuzzled my belly with its feelers.

"Yes," I clicked in its language. "Queen here. Queen mine."

It clicked in sympathy.

A wind from across the mountains swept down into my face. From impossibly far away, it carried the salt of the sea. It carried the scent of the grassland. It carried the rusting metal smell of the derelict, destroyed shapes in the Forbidden Zone.

The wind brought the scent of the distant Hive, sickly and yellow.

And for an instant, so faint I barely registered it, the wind brought the scent of blue.

It wasn't real. Couldn't have been. Even if the Blue Queen larva still lived, there was no way I could possibly smell her from here, a two days walk away. But there was no denying that something inside me was different. I closed my eyes and followed the faint trail left by the Digger from when it came outside this morning ahead of me. I smelled the footsteps where Gil and I had walked in, surrounded by the other people.

More importantly, I smelled the truth.

Everything Mo had told me the night before was real. I had been a slave all my life, a fawning larva desperate for the approval of a species that held no more regard for me than I did for a waterbug. I was not a Lowform. The bugs were not Masters. I was a human, and my people were living a lie.

Mo had said it. They kept the passive ones for breeding. Chen.

My best friend, confined in the bowels of the sickly Yellow Hive for the rest of his life. He wasn't slow. Far from it. But he believed the lie.

The people here had made a plan. The Queen that would have saved us all, the glorious blue-scented Queen, should be here now, incubating on the water beast they called a seal. She should be growing and changing, and calling more soldiers to our cause. Instead she was thrown away, drowned in a vat of algae.

But she wouldn't drown, would she? The eggs were wet. The larvae fed in the water.

Could she possibly be alive?

We had been gone two nights. She would be starving.

The thought twisted my stomach.

I clicked to the Digger guarding me.

"Tonight. I go. Get Queen."

It rubbed my belly with its feelers, tasting the welt the Blue Queen had left. It clicked a question.

"Yes," I answered. "She lives. Must get. You come?"

The bug clicked assent.

CHAPTER 14

NOAH

I slept through the afternoon.

When I woke up in a chamber by myself, the girl Kinni was there with more of the tasteless food. She handed me a little woven basket with strips of the dry stuff in the bottom of it.

"What is this stuff?" I asked her, chewing without enthusiasm.

"It's bat."

I cocked my head. "What's that?"

She rolled her eyes. "The flying things that live in the caves."

The meat was rubbery and bland. I hadn't seen any flying things in the cave where Jerome had died, but there was so much new information racing through my head that the thought didn't have anywhere to go. Of course there were cave things that flew. I'd seen them from the underground rivers, flapping up through holes in the roof when the sun set. Of course this is what they tasted like. Because we were people who came from the stars.

It seemed laughable in the daylight. But everything made sense.

"You ever been out of that Hive before?"

I straightened up. "Of course I was out of the Hive. I'm a great Diver."

She rolled her eyes again, standing in the doorway of the small room. "Great. Getting food for the slavers. That's wonderful." She dropped the woven bowl that held the rest of the meat. "Well, this is bat. It's one of the things we eat. Along with seal and fungus and berries and whatever else we can find wherever we're running from the monsters sent by your precious Queen."

"She's not my Queen," I snapped.

Kinni shrugged. "Fancy words. But I've seen your kind before. Born a slave. We've taken some of your people in the past. We tell them the truth, and they smile and nod, and the first chance they get, they go running back to throw themselves at the feet of your masters. Just like your idiot friend did last night."

My head snapped up. "Gil? Gil went back?"

"Like they all do," she said. "Lexis thinks there's some kind of chemical thing that turns your brains to mush. Makes you stupid. Makes you want to go back to being slaves even after you know what the bugs really are."

The bat meat churned in my belly. "He was as weak as I was. He'll never even make it back."

"Hardly matters. If he dies on the way, fine. If not, they'll kill him as soon as they see him."

I thought about that. Runners had disappeared in my lifetime. None had ever returned. None that I saw. *As if they'd let someone bring that truth back into the Hive.* My face sagged. Kinni was right. The Hive bugs would kill anyone returning. Gil had no chance.

But I had to try. For the Queen.

And I had to be smart about it.

And to do that, I'd need more than just the scarred Digger for help.

CHAPTER 15

NOAH

I descended into the depths of the ruined Hive and found an entry into the river that flowed underneath it. Somewhere in the far distance, the water must connect to the rivers I'd known since I was a child. The river must run all the way under the mountains, through crevasses carved in the rock. My stomach was roiling from the unfamiliar food, and I ached for a familiar taste.

The waterbugs here were easy to catch. I grabbed four of them, smashing them with a rock from the riverbed. On the way back to my room I found Kinni and waved a dead bug in her face.

"Come on. I'll show you what real food tastes like."

She looked like I'd just smeared poop on my face and tried to kiss her. Backing away with a look of horror, she shook her head. "What is that thing? No way!" But she was curious, and she followed me back to my sleeping quarters.

When we got there, I showed her how to peel the shell up and suck the sweet meat from inside.

"Oh, stars, no. No way I'm eating that."

I shrugged. "Didn't think you'd be brave enough. I ate your nasty bat meat, but . . ." I let it trail off as I slurped down the second bug, peeking at her out of the corner of my eye.

She stared at the two remaining bugs. I waited, licking juice off my hands.

"Is it squishy?"

I nodded. "So squishy. So good."

My jibe must have gotten to her, because she picked up one of the bugs. I took the other, and we sucked out the soft meat in tandem.

Her eyes went wide, and her mouth twisted. "Oh, my . . . oh, yuck." She couldn't seem to decide if she wanted to swallow it or spit it out. In the end, she gulped it down, her face still looking wretched.

She stared straight at me. "No matter what else happens in my whole life, there will never be anything as gross as that moment."

I laughed, and after a moment, so did she.

My face turned sober. "I need your help. I'm going to get her back."

Kinni shook her head. "Who? The Queen? It's too late, idiot. You lost her. She's dead."

I wanted to scream at the possibility, but held myself in check. "She might be alive. But she won't be for long. And even if she is, they'll find her and kill her soon."

The thought of them killing her made my throat tighten

up. This girl didn't understand. She hadn't lived in a real Hive, watching the bond among the 'Mites and wishing desperately to be part of it as I always had. And she hadn't touched my Queen. Hadn't shared her blood. There was no way she could possibly understand the sickening grief that shot through me at the thought of my Queen being torn apart. This group of humans and their ways were foreign to me, as I must have been to them. How could I possibly convince her to help me? To help a Queen she'd never even seen?

Honesty. I had nothing else to give.

"Look, you're right. I'm an idiot. I had no idea what was going on, and I want to fix things. But to do that, I need to get back into the Hive, find her, and get her out. I know where she is." *Or was.* "I know how to get in, but I don't know if I'll make it back out. I don't have a plan for that."

She stood up from my sleeping pad and stepped into the doorway, looking over her shoulder. "They won't let you go. They know you'd die, and we need every human we can get."

"Not really, though," I said. "I'm expendable. The Masters—the bugs thought so, anyway."

She brushed a strand of hair out of her eyes and smiled. "That's sure true."

"So anyway, I need to figure out how to get out once I get her."

Kinni re-entered the room and sat on my pile of hides. I plopped down next to her.

"We call them 'Mites."

"What?" That word I didn't know.

"'Mites. The things you call 'Masters.' The insects. Dad says the mounds and tunnels they build are like something called termites from the old planet."

"'Mites." I said. "Right. Well, whatever you call them, they're not going to let me just take her away."

"They probably can't smell her now if you threw her in the vat of algae," she said. "But as soon as you wash her off, they'll smell her for sure. No way to hide. They smell stuff a mile away."

"They do?" I had never wondered about their sense of smell before.

"Of course they do. It's how they get around. They're blind."

I'd like to say my jaw didn't drop, but I'd be lying. *Of course they're blind. They maneuver in total darkness. They stay inside when the pollen storms hit.* I thought about the things I smelled outside that morning. The scent trail left by the outcast bug. The way it had used its feelers on the ring left by the Queen larva. The beautiful blue scent of that ring. I had never smelled anything like those scents before. Something inside me had changed. The Blue Queen had changed me.

"That's the key, then," I said, after too long a pause. "I need to confuse their sense of smell so they can't chase me."

Kinni leaned back against the wall. "They hate the pollen. It confuses them when it hits. Like us in the dark." She looked at the bowl on the floor in the doorway. "We use it when we're traveling close to the Hive. We sprinkle it over our back trail so they can't follow us. Maybe you could . . . . . . I don't know. Sprinkle it over yourself or something? So they couldn't smell you as an outsider, and couldn't smell her?"

"That might work." I sighed. "She's in one of the outside chambers they must have added on. It's got a million tiny holes for sunlight, but nothing big enough for me to get through, even if I could get close enough during a storm."

The next pollen storm wouldn't happen for weeks. My Blue Queen didn't have that kind of time.

"Lexis is working on some kind of explosive," Kinni offered. "We have some weapons we've made, stuff they salvaged from the ships early on, I guess. But she's working on something that you can set on fire and explode."

Those words meant nothing to me.

"Right," I said, trying not to look completely stupid. "I'm not sure if that's the right thing for now."

"No, it's not," she agreed. "She can't really control it. It's just as likely to blow the whole place up, or maybe nothing at all. Can't count on that."

"But back to the pollen idea," I insisted. "I can carry it to the river, no problem. But I need it to stay dry underwater. Do you have something for that?"

She thought a moment. "Maybe. If you took one of the sealskin bags and, maybe . . . covered the seams in wax? That might work. Maybe."

Another word I didn't know. *Wax.*

"Right," I said. "I'm leaving tonight. The Mast—the 'Mite that's supposed to guard me is going to let me go get her. Maybe it will come with me, at least part of the way, in case I get into any trouble. Can you sort out a bag full of pollen with . . . wax . . . for me? Before second moonrise tonight? There's no time to waste."

Kinni shrugged. "I can do that." She stood up and walked over to the bowl, scooping it off the floor. "You're going to die, you know. You'll never make it back."

I knew. But it hardly mattered. I had no Hive. Like the

giant insect in the corridor, I was an outcast. And what did it matter if I died? If my Blue Queen was dead, there was no reason to live another day.

Resolved to my fate, I gave Kinni a weak smile. "You never know. I just might surprise you."

She shrugged again and stalked out of the room.

I pulled the slave tunic off the floor and laid it on the pile of hides. Later tonight, I'd take off these human clothes and put the tunic back on.

Kinni was right. I would probably die. But despite the clothing I had laid out, I would not die a slave.

CHAPTER 16

NOAH

I spent the late evening in the large common room. Everything I'd learned had kept my head spinning the night before, and I'd hardly been able to focus on any of the other people in the dead Hive. Mo seemed to be their leader. He wasn't the strongest or fastest, but everyone seemed to respect him. There were maybe forty humans, and a total of nine outcast bugs, who took turns keeping watch outside overnight. Since I'd learned they were blind and navigated by smell, it made perfect sense for the humans to watch by day, and the bugs by night.

This odd community had lived all over the area, farther than I'd ever dreamed existed. In the early days, the Yellow Queen's Soldiers would patrol from my old Hive, and had destroyed the bugs that built this one. Other abandoned Hives were located all around. But the Yellow Queen was getting old, and the Hive was weakening. They never came this far now, not for years. If I could retrieve the Blue Queen larva, she would be safe here for as long as we needed to build our army.

The larvae that had arrived on Gil's belly would be the start of our own Hive here. But they needed a Queen. We all did. She would hold us together, make us strong.

Kinni had called Gil an idiot. He certainly was, running back to the old Hive even after he knew what they had done to our people. Of all the boys that could have been rescued with me, didn't it just have to be him? He couldn't cope with the truth. Jerome could have handled it.

Poor Jerome. He was so close to freedom. So close to learning who he really was.

But Jerome wasn't here. Neither was Gil now, but that didn't matter. Nothing mattered but finding my Queen.

And what if she's dead? What if you find yourself back in the Hive without her? What will you do?

That wouldn't matter, either. Nothing would matter if she was dead.

When I got back to my room after first moonrise, there were two small, sealed pouches tucked under my old tunic. There was some kind of thin bark with it, with markings on it, which I puzzled over for a few minutes.

"What do you think of my message?" Kinni's voice startled me from the doorway.

"Um . . . thanks for the bags."

She snorted. "Right. The bags. But what about the note?"

Another word I didn't know, but she was looking at the thin bark. I had seen the other humans with thin sheets of bark like this. They seemed to like looking at them and making marks on them. I peered at the markings, which looked like some kind of dark juice in a pattern.

"Um. It's . . . good."

Her eyes rolled to the ceiling. "You can't read, can you?"

Read. There's another new word. Don't let her know. "I can do a lot of things. All kinds of things. You don't know."

"Of course you can," she said, a wicked smile on her face. "So what does it say?"

She pointed at the bark. *What does it say?* I held it up and sniffed it. "It says you were nervous when you made it. Sweating." I grinned. "You don't want me to die, do you?"

Her eyebrows drew together in a scowl. "I couldn't possibly care less." She flounced away down the hallway.

When I was sure she was gone, I held the bark up to my ear. Kinni was crazy. It didn't say anything. It was just bark with juice painted on it.

After second moonrise, I stole out of the dead Hive. The Digger 'Mite that was set to guard me followed along, feelers waving in the air. Kinni had told me this Digger was named Sunshine. She didn't tell me who named it. 'Mites at the old Hive didn't have names. *Did they? Would you have known if they did?*

I hardly needed the guide. Although the scent trail we had left was scant, there were only two low passes through the mountains that divided our side from the Forbidden Zone and my home Hive, and this was the most direct.

Time to stop thinking about it like that. It's not your home. Never really was.

We walked through the night. The Mite's knowledge of the clicking language was scant, and at first I thought this particular insect was not very intelligent. Through the long journey, I figured out that this was not the case at all. Among themselves, the giant insects didn't use the clicks. It was a language developed specifically to communicate with Lowforms . . . human slaves. The 'Mites communicated with scents, following each other's paths and sensing each other's thoughts through the different smells their bodies could make. I had never been able to detect these before, but now the air was alive with them.

There was so much to smell in the darkness. A million kinds of little bugs scampered through the grasses and trees. Warm, furry things flitted through the air and scuttled in burrows underground. When we finally reached the halfway point of the journey, the cave in the hills where Jerome had died, there was no thought of staying there. The stench of his remains and the dead larva that had dropped off his corpse poisoned the air for a mile around it. It seemed cruel to just let him lie there, but no way I could bear to move him.

"Find your star, Jerome," I whispered as I passed, breathing through my mouth, which didn't help at all. It was what Mo had said when he learned we had lost Jerome on the flight from the Hive, and the words had made no sense at the time. But now I knew what stars were.

I looked up at the night sky as we picked our way through the rocky hills. So many stars. Mo had said that some of them weren't even real. They were something called satellites, sent out from the spaceship that brought us here so we would always know where we were. He didn't explain how that was supposed to work, but it didn't matter, because whatever was supposed to help us use those not-stars was lost years ago when the "Mites attacked out of nowhere.

Dawn brightened the sky over the horizon by the time we began our descent. In the far distance, the ocean stretched away forever. The sun hadn't yet risen over its edge, but it wouldn't be long.

"We need to go around." I pointed down into the Forbidden Zone far below. "They patrol there. Can't get caught." I spoke in the human language, but Sunshine seemed to understand my meaning.

We picked a new path, skirting down the hills to the south of the Hive. A thick forest rimmed the edge of the huge field, and we stayed deep in the tree line.

The sun was well up before I found what I was looking for. An open patch of blue sky looked down onto bare rock with a deep hole in the middle. Below ground, the river flowed toward the Hive. I had never ventured this far in the underground river, but trusted my sense of direction to lead me in.

Sunshine's great strength allowed it to shove a small downed tree halfway over the edge of the sinkhole. If I made it back to this pocket, I'd be able to climb out.

I was exhausted by the night's travel, but too excited to nap as I'd planned. A rest would do me good, but there was no point in trying.

I checked the bindings on the waxed pouches tied around my waist under my tunic.

"Wait. One day. I come. Or no."

The 'Mite clicked understanding. In one day's time, I would either return victorious, or not at all.

I clicked out the 'Mite words for "Goodbye," which

literally translated to: "Eat well."

With a great, heaving breath, I jumped into the cold, flowing water and descended into the current.

CHAPTER 17

KINNI

"He did what?"

My dad looked like the top of his head might blow off. I had thought about pleading ignorance when the idiot boy Noah was missed at breakfast, but Dad raised me to be truthful.

"He left," I repeated. "He thinks the Queen larva might still be alive. He's going back to try and get her."

Dad paced around the main hall. Most of our people were out before dawn, hunting for food and gathering anything we could use in the bug-house.

"When did he leave?"

I shrugged. "Sometime after second moonrise, I expect. He took Sunshine with him."

The 'Mites didn't have names of their own. Apparently that wasn't a thing in bug-life. So when they showed up, somebody would think of a name so we could keep them straight. Not that it mattered. They were all the same. Huge, stupid, blind bugs with no independent thoughts, some with a tail that could take down anything on the planet. They were strong and easy to boss around. Used to doing what they were told. The ones that came from the Slaver's Hive all understood the clicking language that was the only kind of sound they could make. A few that had drifted in from farther away couldn't even do that, although some of them learned in time.

Dad was royally pissed off. "He's gonna get himself killed. And if he doesn't, he's gonna lead them straight back here to us. What's he thinking, getting close to the Slave Hive when there's not a pollen storm happening?"

"How would he know any better?" I countered. "He's literally been a slave his whole life, and he didn't even know it until yesterday." Why was I standing up for him? He was an idiot, like every other idiot we'd tried to rescue.

"But we told him," Dad said. "We told him the whole story. He knows now. Why would he do this?"

I grabbed a strip of dried bat from the line where we hung meat. "He seemed kind of crazy. Kept rubbing the spot on his belly where he thinks the Queen was sucked onto him. I swear, it's some kind of chemical thing. Pheromones or something, like Lexis says. Anybody that comes out of that Hive is just not right in the head."

Not that this Hive was any better. This place had been abandoned generations ago, when the Slaver Queen wiped out all the bugs anywhere near her. It was one of many places I'd lived in my fourteen years. Wasn't safe to stay anywhere for long. The Soldiers hadn't come after us for a long time, and I hoped what Dad said about the Slave Hive was true. That the Queen was old and sick and would die soon. We didn't know what would happen to a Hive that didn't have a Queen, but if the bugs around here were any indication, they'd probably just wander around and look sad all the time. If nobody told them to do something, they didn't do anything. *Bunch of stupid bugs.*

Dad seemed to come to a decision. He looked around the hive at the few people that were getting breakfast and starting their day's chores.

"We move out tonight."

Oh no. That was even stupider than the idiot going back to the Slave Hive.

"Dad, we can't. We never move except at pollen time. They might smell us."

"We have to take that risk." He peered out one of the little holes in the ceiling at the gray sky. Some days were bright blue, and others were a dusty, shifting gray. Dad said it was something to do with an asteroid cloud. Today was a light gray day. "We'll gather our things and head up into the mountain camp at dawn tomorrow."

"What about the maggots in the basement?"

He ran a hand through what was left of his hair. "Blast it. We can't leave them. We'll need them."

A couple of the older men offered to stay with them.

Dad nodded. "Yes, I think a few people should stay. If somehow Noah manages to get back with the Queen larva, he won't know where we've gone. I'll stay here with a couple of men and the 'Mites to guard the larvae. Everyone else will head to the mountain camp. Next pollen time, we'll come back and see where things lie."

"I'm staying too—" I began, but Dad cut me off.

"No way. You're far too valuable. You'll go up the mountain with the rest and wait. We'll join you when Noah comes back."

He didn't look hopeful, and I started to doubt whether I should have let the boy go. But what would it matter? There weren't enough of us humans to keep a population going. We were never going to get the rest of the people rescued from the Slave Hive. It was a pipe dream. In another thirty years or so, the only humans left alive on this forsaken planet would be slaves to the 'Mites. They'd survive, but would they still be humans? Not really. Humans didn't live like that.

Part of the old legend that Dad hadn't included last night was the bit about the other ships. We were supposed to have come down from a spaceship called the Horizon Beta. If the legend was true, there were two others out there. The Alpha should have landed on its planet a couple of years ago, by Dad's figuring.

I hoped they were doing better than we were. If the fate of the human race was up to the pathetic descendants of the Beta, I didn't hold much hope for our species.

CHAPTER 18

NOAH

I took a huge breath and plunged under the water. No Diver had ever been this far from the Hive. The light from the open sinkhole didn't penetrate far, and I had no way to know how far downstream I might find another air pocket to breathe. If it was too far, I would drown. My body would wash on down the black river, past the Hive where my people were held as slaves, and on out to sea. No one would find me, and no one would miss me.

She would. My Queen.

If I drowned, she would never know. She would die, too, starved to death in the algae tank where I'd wiped her away.

If she hasn't already.

I argued with myself as I kicked downstream. Here and there, tiny cracks in the ceiling allowed pinpoints of light to shine down through the crystal clear water. Without any sense of smell to guide me, only those shafts of light showed me the way. But I was never lost in the water. I ducked under a steep overhang and came up in a sunlit pool, gasping for air.

Four of the water beasts that the humans called seals grazed in the shallows.

"Stay away from the Hive," I warned them, as if they might understand. "They'll suck you dry. Just like us."

In a moment, I was re-oriented. The section of river I had just come down had taxed my lungs. And coming back, if I came back, I'd be swimming upstream instead of down.

Once more I ducked into the icy flow. The river forked, and I went left. Another air hole was just large enough to push my face out of the water and grab a breath, fingers scrabbling to hold on to the underside of the rock.

You're going to die.

I shoved the voice away, sucked in air, and descended.

Twice I chose the wrong path and had to double back when the walls closed in too tight to admit my body. I clawed my way back upstream and chose a different tunnel, marking the way in my memory.

Slowly, the caverns began to feel familiar. By the time I reached the sunny pool where I had collected waterbugs for the Ranking, I knew I would make it. But this was only half of the journey. The easy half.

I didn't want to emerge in the main pool where the 'Mites sent humans into the water to fetch their food. Instead, I turned left and headed for a different area that I knew must lead under the Hive, into the area beyond the Boundary, where humans weren't allowed.

When I surfaced into the familiar darkness of the deep

tunnels, I nearly retched at the smell.

Sickly and yellow, the stench of the aging Queen and her dying Hive was overpowering. How had I never smelled this before? How had I lived in this horrific stench my whole life? How did anyone survive here?

I crawled from the water and checked the bags of pollen under my slave tunic. The wax felt intact, but there was no way to know if the pollen inside had stayed dry. If it came out in a big, wet clump, I'd be dead for sure.

So many ways to die here. And only one way to live.

On the journey across the hills, I had worried that I might smell different to the 'Mites in this Hive. In total darkness, I should have been lost and alone down here. But the corridor was awash in scent trails. Kneeling on the hard ground, I took a big sniff. 'Mites had traveled this path, though not recently. They left a faint, moist trail as they went. I had never realized.

I rolled in the scent trail, grinding my wet tunic into every trace of the sick yellow stench I could find. If Kinni was right and the 'Mites really were blind, I was now invisible. At least, I hoped so.

But the humans would see me. As soon as I emerged from beyond the boundary, I was certain to run into someone. Dung-scrapers or Gardeners would be about. I pulled my hair down over my face and slumped my shoulders, eyes on the floor.

Outside one of the fungus gardens, I found a large, empty basket, which I grabbed and held in front of me. I walked quickly, with purpose, as if I had somewhere to be.

The humans I passed didn't even glance up from their own work. The 'Mites waved a feeler in my direction before scuttling away on their own business.

Up and up I climbed, staying to the outside edges of the Hive's tunnels. I could feel the hated Yellow Queen below me, wafting out sickness and decay. This Hive was doomed, but they couldn't see it. Most of them, anyway. For the first time, I thought about the 'Mites that had pulled me and the other boys out of the pools instead of stinging us as they should have. They must understand what was happening there. Somehow they must have made contact with the free humans and agreed to the plan, to save a new Queen larva before the old Queen could have her killed. Surely they realized it was best for all of us if this succeeded. But I didn't know which 'Mites they were, or if they were still in the Hive. I'd been so dazed and sick from the paralyzing venom, I hadn't stopped to try and recognize which ones they were.

No matter. This was my mission. No one could help me.

By the time I reached the corridor that led to the outer chamber where the vats of algae were, it was late in the evening. 'Mites skittered around, and the last few human slaves stood in line for their bowls of the slime I now knew had been taken from one of the transports that brought our people down from space. I felt stupid for never realizing that the vats were clearly not made of anything the 'Mites could produce. But I hadn't called them 'Mites then. They were Masters to me.

One of them stood in the doorway to the algae room. I would have to pass right by it to get inside.

Calm. It will smell fear.

Deep breaths.

I crowded right into the back of the man in front of me and pushed past the 'Mite in the doorway. If it realized

I didn't belong, I'd be trapped in here. There was only one doorway out.

We circled around the vats, each man scooping out a bowl of algae. I was last in line.

Was she here? I couldn't smell her. My heart pounded at the thought that she might be alive, just an arm's length away. It pounded harder at the thought that she might be dead.

At the far end of the room, I dropped my bowl on the floor. The vats sat on thick legs, and there was just enough room to slide my body underneath the farthest one.

Breathe. Calm. Don't make a sound.

I couldn't see a thing, lying flat on my back under the vat. If the man in front of me realized I was gone, it would all end right now.

I listened. The 'Mite in the doorway gave out the last of the shellfish, harvested that day by Divers in the sea. It scuttled around the outside of the vats. I held my breath.

No one here. Just the sick, rotten stench of your dying Hive.

It paused on the far side and I willed my heart to stop beating so loudly.

It skittered away.

Long moments I waited, lying on the cold, hard ground, my chest pushed against the underside of the vat.

The room grew dark. No one would come in here until morning.

I crept out from under the vat and crouched behind it. I was alone.

Three giant vats sat in the room. I had wiped all the larvae off me into the one nearest the doorway. I crept over to it now and plunged my hands inside. Sweeping them from side to side, I let the thick slime pass through my fingers.

Nothing.

Despair gripped my chest. She had to be here. She had to be alive.

I couldn't reach the bottom of the vat leaning over the side. I stripped off my wet tunic, pulled the bags of pollen from my waist, and vaulted over the edge into the algae. My toes slid along the bottom, searching for anything solid in the slimy tank.

Something was there.

My hands plunged down and closed around a fat, wriggling, soft shape. The moment I touched it, my heart burst into song.

I pulled her from the slime. She was as long and fat as my thigh, shiny and beautiful. The green slime clung to her and she sucked it up into her perfect mouth.

"You love the algae?" I purred to her. "You're so nice and fat, you beautiful thing. Did you eat all the other larvae?" Of course she did. She was the Blue Queen. It was only right.

I held her to my belly and she latched on, covering the tiny ring she'd made only days ago with a much larger mouth. As soon as she connected, a wave of ecstasy flowed through my whole body and I shivered with joy.

"I've found you, my Queen. And I'll never let you go."

CHAPTER 19

NOAH

I could have stayed there forever, wallowing in the glory of my connection to the Queen. Even in the midst of all that sick yellow stench, having her against my skin, sharing my blood, was electrifying. But there was no time to revel in my incredible good fortune. The Queen was still covered by a layer of green algae slime, but her scent would soon be a beacon to every 'Mite for miles around. I dunked my tunic right into the vat and pulled it over my head, squishing the algae all around the bulge that she made. In each hand I held one of the bags of pollen, which I re-tied to the cord around my waist.

"Time to go home, my Queen."

The Hive was quiet, but I had no illusion that I could walk unmolested out the entrance. Most of the 'Mites and all of the humans would be down below in their sleeping chambers, but Soldiers would patrol inside and outside all night long, and Diggers and Builders were always at work. If they smelled us, we could never outrun them.

I slipped out of the algae room and into the corridor. A few scattered glowstones lit the path, but I didn't need them. Scent trails on the floor told me the story of every human and 'Mite that had passed through these hallways. Still, I grabbed a basket of them and held them under the large bulge under the front of my tunic. It supported the Queen's surprising weight and took the pressure off her hold on my belly, which was starting to hurt. My feet were silent, padding along the dim tunnels.

When I passed the turnoff to where the human females were kept, I paused. There would be 'Mite guards right down the hall. I had always thought they were there to protect the mothers and babies, and perhaps they were. But now I knew they were also there to keep anyone from escaping.

Chen was down there somewhere. How could I be this close, knowing the truth of our existence, and not try to rescue him? I stood there at the crossroad, taking quiet breaths. Could I blind the 'Mites' sense of smell with the pollen, rush in, and grab Chen? Would he follow me without question, as I needed him to do? He probably would. The life of a Caretaker male was a horror, stuck in the dark underground forever. Once a boy became a Caretaker, he was never seen in the Hive again. *Just like Queen's Service.* Was he still alive? How many Caretaker males were there? One or two got chosen every Ranking, and when I thought about this I realized they couldn't be Caretakers for very long. We could live twenty or thirty years, and there wasn't room for hundreds of adult male humans. And there wasn't a need. The 'Mites were very efficient at serving the Hive's needs. What happened to them once their time was up?

As if I didn't know.

But I couldn't take him with me now. Chen wasn't a strong enough swimmer, and our lives would depend on kicking upstream in the underground river farther than I'd ever gone before. I might not make it. Chen would never survive.

I'll be back for you. Soon.

I scuttled away down the corridor.

I'd been lucky so far, but as the algae started to dry up around the Queen, her perfect blue scent was becoming evident. 'Mites would smell her if I could. I ducked down a passageway toward an off-limits area. A large, falling sky-rock had caused a collapse of a small part of the western part of the Hive a few weeks ago, and Builders would be shoring it up while Diggers removed the debris. It was a calculated risk. There would probably be more 'Mites in that area, but they wouldn't be Soldiers. Diggers could snap me in half with their huge claws, but they were slow and methodical in their work. Builders might bite off a limb, but one sting from a Soldier and this rescue would be over.

Glow stones in my basket lit the way. Through the bond of my blood, I could feel the Queen's displeasure as the algae coating dried, pulling on her delicate skin. Her scent went from pure blue to a veined purple. *Just a little ways farther and we'll be in the water.* I couldn't speak to her out loud, but I hoped she might feel my intention.

I turned a corner and ran straight into a Builder. It was spitting out the chewed wood and dirt that built our Hive, cementing a fallen area back into place. Just past it, fresh air drifted into the Hive and I sucked at the absence of the Yellow Queen's stench.

The Builder froze. It scuttled around in place to face me, jaws working at the last bits of pulp and mud. Its feelers vibrated on the top of its head, waving in my direction.

"Sorry," I clicked, and scooted past. It didn't follow right away, but after a few steps, the sound of its feet on the hard clay ticked up behind me. The soft feelers caressed the back of my neck and I shivered.

It smells her. It has to.

But maybe it didn't know what the smell meant.

Another Builder cut me off at the end of the hallway, scuttling in my direction. The one behind me didn't attack, merely following me and tickling me with its soft antennae.

Every nerve in my body screamed, "Run." But if I ran, they would know for sure. They would raise the alarm, and I'd be surrounded. I continued walking forward, eyes downcast like any Lowform. When I reached the Builder 'Mite blocking my path, I clicked, "I pass," the 'Mite way to say "Excuse me," and tried to sidle past. It let me, but joined the other in rubbing its antennae around me.

They smell her. And they like it.

Could it be this easy? Would the mere presence of this lovely baby Queen turn the Hive? Would they all follow her and we could end this without death on either side? For a few moments, it seemed like the answer might be "yes."

Then the Soldiers arrived.

They weren't enthralled by the Blue Queen's scent. They were enraged by it.

Three of them charged up from behind us, shoving at the Builders that trailed behind me. I flung the basket behind me and bolted ahead.

Another Soldier dashed in from a side hallway and I veered around it, throwing myself against the wall, which sent a shower of dirt down around us and made the Soldiers behind me pause.

Fool. Throw the pollen!

I ripped the first bag out from under my tunic and tore off the wax seal, tossing the bag into the air behind me. The hoped-for puff of red pollen didn't happen. Just a wet plop as the soggy mass inside splatted on the floor.

Oh, moons, here we go. I'm sorry, my Queen.

The second bag wouldn't rip off the cord that held it, and I fumbled with the knot as I ran. The Soldiers were steps behind me, close enough that I could hear their huge lungs pumping.

I ripped off the seal and tossed the bag.

The air filled with thick, red, floral-scented debris.

Two of the Soldiers chasing me crashed into each other, and the two that were running behind stumbled into them, tumbling into a mass of legs and stinging tails. I dashed forward out of the noxious cloud, as disoriented as they were with the pollen destroying my new sense of smell.

Up ahead, starlight glittered through a hole in the Hive wall.

I bolted for it, flying faster than I ever thought I could run. The Soldiers behind me had regained their feet, and I smelled the distress signal they emitted, yellow-orange with rage. In a few moments, every Soldier from the Hive would be racing this way.

A Digger scuttled into the opening, waving its huge claws.

"Move!" I clicked, hoping to the stars that it would listen.

It moved. As I flew past, it reached out with its antennae to get a taste of the Blue Queen, but I was moving far too fast. I vaulted over a low wall that hadn't collapsed, and emerged into the moonlight. My feet pounded on the hard ground, and from all around me came the sound of Soldier 'Mites on the hunt.

CHAPTER 20

NOAH

In the moonlight, I thought I might have a slight advantage. If Mo was telling the truth, the 'Mites had no vision, and relied completely on smell to navigate. They were so good at it that I never suspected they couldn't see. And I had no idea what had changed inside me that I could smell things I never had before, but it must have had something to do with sharing the Queen's blood. Was my sense of smell as strong as theirs now? No idea, but in the moonlight, I had a gray, dim vision.

I almost wished I didn't. Soldiers rushed at me from both sides and behind, pouring out of the Hive. I had a small head start, but Soldiers could skitter on their six hind legs faster than I could run on two. In a flat-out footrace, I was outclassed. And there was nowhere to hide. As the algae dried and cracked, the Blue Queen's angry purple scent filled the night. Every 'Mite for miles would know where she was.

The ground was rocky as I crested the hillside and flew down toward the grassland. My lungs burned with the effort, and the Queen's anger at being bounced around was making me nauseous.

You're a fool. You've doomed her.

I risked a peek over my shoulder. Soldiers everywhere, and in front of the pack, the two Diggers that had been the first to realize what I was smuggling under my tunic. They ran faster than I ever thought Diggers could run, outpacing even the Soldiers.

They feel it. She calls to them.

I stumbled at the bottom of the hill and caught my footing, rushing out onto the grassland. Here and there, pockets of trees and brush stood out as black spots in the dim light. Could I possibly hide in one of them?

The smell of water drew me to the left. A large copse of trees was a shadow straight ahead of me. I bolted for it, though I knew nothing there could possibly hide the Queen's scent, or the trail my footsteps were leaving as I ran. When I reached the little patch of plant life, I pulled up short.

Through a small crack in the ground came the smell of fresh water. I was above one of the many cracks that let light into the underground rivers. This was not a section I had ever dived in before, but there was no doubt that below me was a branch of the river.

The two Diggers crashed into the bushes.

"Dig! Help Queen!" I clicked at them, praying they were among the 'Mites that understood the language.

They paused for a moment, then tore into the rocks at my feet with their huge claws. Dirt and stones flew as they worked in a fever, spurred by the urgency in my tone. I had no idea what they were thinking. They couldn't see me. Did they think the order came from the Blue Queen? Did they realize she was just a larva, not even pupated yet? Did it matter?

Soldiers pounded toward us and the crack at my feet widened. Far below, the sound of the rushing water flowed by, echoing in what must be a large, open cavern under this thin ceiling of rock. The hole was almost large enough for me to slip into, but it had to be big enough that the Queen on my belly wouldn't be scraped off as I squeezed through.

"Hurry! Fast! Help Queen!"

They dug with a frenzy.

As the first Soldier burst into the brush, tail raised to strike, I shoved the Diggers out of my way and jammed my legs into the hole. I turned so that the largest opening was at my front, and pulled myself downward through the narrow crack, rocks scraping skin from my sides. My feet hung over nothing and I shimmied my shoulders down through the hole.

Almost there. We're going to make it.

My tunic snagged on a sharp rock and pulled over my head.

I dangled there, hung by the cloth, twisting and kicking to free myself. My left arm was stuck in the hole and I couldn't break free.

One of the Diggers grabbed at me. Did it think it could save me and pull me up? Its sharp claw tore the tunic away from the rock, and I fell.

Images flashed through my mind as I plunged into darkness.

Some of the larger rock caverns were just openings from the river straight up to the ceiling, with plain rock walls and nothing but water underneath. Others had small beaches where the rock curved down to the water's edge, leaving a flat, solid surface on which plant life thrived. I had no idea which kind of cavern this was. If it was the first kind, I was about to splash into freezing water.

If it was the second, I was about to crush all my bones on the rocky ledge next to the river's flow.

My brain processed this in an instant's panic as the light from above dwindled in my vision.

The water hit me almost as hard as rocks would have. All my breath was stolen as the icy splash pounded into my back. My arms were wrapped around the Queen, and I plunged into black water. How deep? Was I about to impale myself on the jagged bottom? I kicked hard for the surface.

The river moved fast here, and as my head broke from the water, my back slammed into a jut of rock. The current held me fast and I scrambled to keep my head above water. I was still in the large, open cavern.

And the Diggers were still digging.

Whether they were trying to get to the Queen for their own reasons, or acting at the behest of the Soldiers, I didn't know or care. In the moments that I clawed at the rocks around me, gasping for painful breaths, more and more moonlight streamed into the hole.

Shadows covered it, and suddenly it was raining Soldiers.

They dropped into the cavern, heedless of the fact that they couldn't swim. I darted to the side as the first two were pulled past me, staying out of range of their stingers, carried in the current. More and more piled in, and as they fell, they bounced off each other. There was enough light now to see that the rock I was hanging onto was an outcropping from one of those flat ledges.

Soldiers scrambled out of the water, up onto the ledge and rushed toward me.

I didn't dare just let go and flow with the current. The water downstream was clogged with drowning Soldiers.

"We have to swim. Hang on," I murmured to the Queen on my belly. Without the tunic to support her, only the grasp of her mouth on my skin kept her from being swept away. I wanted to hold onto her body, but I would need both hands to get us out of this chamber.

I ducked under the water and swam for our lives. The river was narrow here, water rushing right at me, and as I kicked under the open patch of moonlight, a Soldier dropped into the water right on top of me. Its legs grasped at me and I kicked it away, waiting for the sting that would end this pathetic rescue. But the Soldier's grip let go, and it tumbled away behind me.

Swim. Swim like never before.

The cavern ended in a black tunnel where the river flowed in. Somewhere up ahead would be another cavern like this one, or an air hole crack to the surface. How far was it? No way to tell.

At the upstream edge, I grabbed onto a lip of rock and took a huge breath, sides heaving with pain.

I submerged into the black tunnel, and kicked into the darkness.

CHAPTER 21

NOAH

The first leg of the swim was mercifully short. I pulled myself forward against the current through a narrow passage with rock all around me. This part of the river system was completely foreign to me. Another air hole could be just ahead, or a mile away. My eyes strained in the darkness, searching for a tiny ray of moonlight streaming down into the water that would tell me a crack led to the surface. To air.

I found one quickly, a hole in the rock ceiling just large enough to cram my face into, pulling deep breaths of still, warm air. My fingers gripped the sides of the hole, keeping me in place against the current.

What do I do now?

I was stuck in a system of caves flooded with rushing water, with no idea where I was. My sense of direction told me which way I wanted to head, but with no knowledge of this part of the river, I could easily choose the wrong passage, one without air holes. I could drown like so many Divers before me, washed away to the sea. No one would know. No one would care. My Queen would die with me.

The hole I held onto was far too small to consider shimmying up.

What if I let go and flowed back down the way I came? Surely the Soldiers had given up by now. They couldn't possibly smell the Queen from where she hung on my belly underwater. I couldn't smell her. If I drifted back to the chamber where I came in, could I possibly climb out? How long would it take them to smell her and come for us if I did?

Scrabbling feet overhead made dirt fall into my open mouth.

They were here.

I smelled them overhead, running across the ground high above me. They weren't digging at the top of my airhole, so I knew they didn't know where I was. But they were searching for me. For her. For us. No way I could possibly risk going backwards. They'd be waiting for sure.

And the cold water was already starting to sap my energy, pulling away my strength and my heat.

Also, there's a big fat 'Mite larva sucked onto your stomach. She's not doing you any favors there. But there was no thought of peeling her off me. I could no more consign her to certain death than fly up to the spaceship that Mo had assured me was somewhere high overhead in the night sky, one of the many blinking stars I had never questioned. She was taking my energy, but I would give her everything I had.

We're together. Live or die, we stay together.

I spit out the dirt, took another deep breath, and pushed

off the air hole.

Turn right. Duck under. Light ahead. Rest.

The next air hole was tiny, just big enough to stick my lips into, sucking the damp air from above. My head couldn't come out of the water, and I didn't hear any Soldiers, but who knew how far they would chase us?

Push off. Swim hard. Three tunnels ahead. I chose the largest one, where the current was weakest.

I was rewarded with another large, open cavern. Multiple small cracks in its distant ceiling let in the moonlight and precious air, and I held onto a rock ledge, lungs pumping. Everything hurt. My sides were skinned by the squeeze through the hole when I dropped. My ribs were beaten by the fall into the water. My belly ached where the Queen held on for her life.

"Be brave, my Queen," I whispered, loud in the open chamber. "I'm going to get you home."

A couple of the water beasts—seals—nudged into my legs. Their warm, furry bodies spun and wove around me, splashing in the water.

"Not now," I muttered, shoving them away. They looked at me with sad brown eyes, and tumbled away down the river.

I rested as long as I dared. But each passing moment stole more of my waning strength.

Go now, or you'll never make it.

I had to be close to where Sunshine waited, assuming the scarred Digger was still there. I closed my eyes and re-oriented myself. *It has to be to the right.*

Cold water closed around me as I pushed myself back out into the smooth current.

Just one more swim. Surely just one more.

The tunnel led in the direction I wanted to go. It had to be a branch I hadn't chosen on my swim to the Hive.

Exhaustion was catching up to me. How long since I'd slept? Not today. Not yesterday.

And not tomorrow if you don't hurry up. Or maybe . . . tomorrow and forever if you don't hurry up.

The Queen on my belly was content in the cold water, but I was nearly used up.

"Here we go."

I ducked under the water and kicked with all I had. The tunnel widened, but no light shone through the solid rock ceiling, which sloped down deeper and deeper. I swam as panic grew inside me.

My lungs burned. My throat ached to open.

The tunnel leveled out, but much too deep. No air holes down here. If it didn't slope back up fast, we were done for.

Just a little farther. Little farther. Little farther. The words lost meaning, echoing in my head.

I couldn't do it. The cold, the fear, and the life-sucking Queen had taken too much for me. My arms relaxed.

Just breathe. One big breath of water and it's all done. You did your best.

My legs stopped kicking.

I'm sorry. So sorry.

Like a bolt of lightning, pain and strength blasted through my belly. Jolted out of my stupor, I clawed at the water around me, scrambling against the current in an electric frenzy.

The tunnel sloped up and I pushed my feet against the wall, shooting for the surface. Gray light filtered in.

With a great, heaving breath, I surfaced in the dim cavern. I clawed my way to the air, and hung there half in the water, retching up foam. Shivers gripped all my muscles and my fingers lost their grip on the edge. For a moment I hung at the edge of the river. Then a giant claw reached down and grabbed the back of my pants, hauling me out onto the rock ledge.

Soft, feathery feelers caressed the larva on my skin.

"We made it, Sunshine," I whispered. "Meet your new Queen."

CHAPTER 22

NOAH

The walk home was a blur. Before we left the cavern I pulled some of the large leaf fronds from under the water and wrapped them around the Queen to keep her moist. We'd need to make good time back to our dead Hive so she wouldn't dry out, but my legs were jellyfish. Sunshine picked me up in its giant claws and carried me most of the way.

We paused at a stream in the mountains to wet down the leaves wrapping the Queen. I took a deep drink but threw it right back up. I had barely eaten for days now, and the Queen was taking what little reserve I had left.

"No down. No curl."

Sunshine knew a lot of our shared language. It wanted me to stay awake, apparently worried that if I fell asleep, I would die, or "curl," as the 'Mites did when they died.

"I won't. I'm okay."

But my mind was drifting. The long swim with the Queen had taken so much out of me, and although I knew she had spurred me on through the last tunnel with her own strength, mine flagged as she continued to suck my blood.

"No sleep. Hear."

It took most of the journey for Sunshine to tell me its story. There were so many words it didn't know, and I had to guess, speaking in the human language it seemed to understand but was unable to speak.

I pieced it together, and as I parsed through the tale, it came alive in my exhausted brain. Sunshine ceased to be an "it" to me, but a "him," just like me and my friends back at the Hive.

He was hatched and molted in a Hive far to the north of the one where I had lived. His Queen was young and healthy, and the Hive thrived. While Sunshine and the other Diggers were excavating a new tunnel, a heavy rain came and caved it in. They worked on the surface, clearing out the rubble so that a new tunnel could be dug.

That's when he smelled the human.

Their Hive was so far from the one where I had grown up that they had never seen the humans I called Ferals. They had no idea what such a creature could be. But Sunshine knew it was something different. The Soldiers guarding the Diggers at work noticed it, too, but no one knew what to make of it.

They learned.

When the pollen storm came, most of the Hive went dormant for the two days of blindness as the pollen destroyed their sense of smell. That's when my Hive attacked.

It was long before I was born. I wouldn't have known

any of the Runners they used.

Sunshine's Hive never knew what hit them.

My Hive . . . the Slave Hive, as Kinni called it, used the Runners as scouts. They found Sunshine's Hive and learned the route. Soldiers from the Slave Hive, blind in the pollen storm, were led by those Runners right up to Sunshine's Hive, invisible to any 'Mites inside. They burst in every entrance, massacring the Soldiers in their dormant state.

The Runners came in first. None of them survived the attack.

Every 'Mite in the Hive fought for their Queen, but in the end, a bunch of Diggers and Builders were no match for the Slave Hive's Soldiers. They fell in the hundreds. Sunshine was one of the last survivors. He fell back to the tunnels surrounding his Queen. He would have died rather than leave her.

The Soldiers poured down the tunnel. Nearly every Digger and Builder was killed. Sunshine blocked the last tunnel to his Queen, wedging his body into the gap.

They stung him and he went limp. As he witnessed, paralyzed and helpless, the Soldiers dragged him out of the tunnel, nearly severing his left claw. They sent one single Soldier into the Queen's chamber.

Sunshine was paralyzed, but his senses were alert. When they killed his Queen, he was among the only members of her Hive alive to smell her terror and her death.

The Soldiers returned to the upper chambers of the Hive to wait out the rest of the pollen storm, unable to return since their guides all died in the fighting.

In the deepest chamber of the Hive, Sunshine's paralysis began to wear off. The Soldiers had nearly used up their venom by the time they reached him, and he didn't get a full dose. Only that saved his life.

But he didn't care. He limped into the tunnel, dragging his injured claw under his belly. Inside the Queen's chambers, he stopped, overwhelmed with grief. She lay still, arms curled around her body in death. Her tiny King, father to every member of the Hive, lay in front of her, his limbs ripped from his body.

Sunshine crawled over the dead King and buried his head in the dead Queen's cold embrace. His feelers stroked her lifeless body. The last of the oil from her gland, the blessing she bestowed onto her beloved Hive, congealed on her skin. He rubbed it into his own head, grief overcoming him as he tasted the final communion with her.

When he finally emerged from the Queen's Chamber and stumbled through the tunnels, the enemy Soldiers were gone. A few survivors from his Hive drifted through the depths, lost without the guidance of a Queen. The stench of her dying agony filled the Hive, and by the next pollen storm, every member of his destroyed Hive had left it, wandering in the wilderness. There was no other Hive to accept them. Every 'Mite along the coast had fallen to the Slave Hive's Soldiers.

A 'Mite without a Hive wouldn't last long. Without a Queen, there was no Hive. Sunshine didn't eat, didn't sleep. His need for a Queen led him aimlessly across the low mountain passes.

Feral humans found him. A few 'Mites from the Slave Hive, those injured or sick and cast out, had already found refuge with the unlikeliest of communities. Sunshine recognized the underlying human scent and recoiled, but these humans didn't smell of the Slave Hive.

They took him in. Fed him. The other 'Mites taught him the clicking language to communicate with the humans.

There was no Queen. It was not a real Hive. But it was enough, just barely, to give him enough purpose to go on.

'Mites had no word for "revenge." But Sunshine understood it. He longed for it. For his decimated Hive and long-dead Queen, he would live to fight for it.

The huge Digger carried me and our larval Queen across the pass and down into the shadow of the hills. I drifted in and out of wakefulness, dreaming confused, fitful dreams. I was in a tunnel and the Soldiers were coming. I was in the water and there were no air holes. I was deep in a hole and the walls were caving in around me. Sunshine never wavered. He plodded on through the night, holding me in his damaged claw. Late the next afternoon I felt hands pulling me from the Digger's claws, carrying me into the Hive. Down into the dank, empty tunnels we went, my eyes seeing nothing and my nose telling me we were almost there.

Rough fingers pried under the Queen's mouth, detaching her from my skin.

"No!" I screamed, grabbing at her as they pulled her away from me. Blood seeped from the round wound on my belly, empty without her weight. How could they take her from me? She was mine. I was hers. I lunged with all my strength, and flopped onto the rocks. My hands reached out for her, but they took her to the emaciated seal in the pool and she latched onto it next to the rest of the larvae.

"Please, bring her back," I murmured, and blackness took me.

CHAPTER 23

CHEN

I had been down in the Waiting Hall for two days.

That's what we called it. Not the Mothers' Chambers, although it was full of mothers. All the female Lowforms lived here, raising babies to do the work of the Hive.

That work would one day save us all.

I missed the daylight, the feeling of warm sun on my shoulders. I missed my friends, but they would all be split up by now, gone to their jobs all over the Hive. I missed Noah, but consoled myself thinking he had surely made Diver and was out in the sea somewhere providing for us, or deep in the tunnels of water he loved so much.

My sisters were overjoyed to have me in their lives. It felt a bit strange to suddenly have family. Even the concept of "family" was unfamiliar to me. Lowforms were never really part of the Hive, and we boys had no idea about any shared bloodlines we might have. But my sisters knew. The women in the Waiting Hall remembered every boy that had ever been taken into the Hive. The more I learned, the happier I was to be back with them in the deep tunnels.

The first night I got here, they sat me down and told me the truth. My sisters Glenna and Shari sat on either side of me, with everyone else clustered around. Their eyes all glazed over as Shari told the story, reveling in the history of our people.

"We came from the stars," Shari said.

I glanced up to where the sunlight came through a tiny hole in the ceiling. Could they even see stars down here?

She continued. "Our people were angels once. We flew through the night sky on long, starlit wings. The sun was our food and the moons were our playthings. We were nothing like these dirty shells that trap us now." She rubbed her own skin and the people around shook their heads.

I said nothing, and Shari went on.

"But we became callous. Unkind to each other. Instead of sharing the gifts of the universe, we became jealous and vengeful. We ruined a planet full of life and hope, and flew away into the sky, laughing about our broken toy."

The looks on people's faces made me squirm on the ground. None of this made a bit of sense to me, but they felt it so strongly, heads bowed in shame for some crime I couldn't even imagine.

Shari looked around at the group. "And so we were punished."

A shiver ran down my spine. I was punished, for sure. I listened more closely to her story.

"We were cast down from the sky, our wings broken

on the ground. We were crushed into these soft bodies, and left to die in our shame. The Masters found us there, weeping for our lost glory. They brought us here, to the deep underground, far from the stars that once fed us, and locked us away in darkness."

Tears filled the eyes of some of the people listening.

"At first we raged against the Masters. We fought with all we had, but these bodies are nothing compared to their strength. And slowly we realized the truth."

I leaned forward. Truth. I needed to know the truth.

"We were punished, and sent down from the skies. And we are punished still. These walls that hold us are not a prison," she said, gesturing to the thick brown walls around us. "They are a safety. We need time to reflect. To understand our shame. The Masters have given us the chance to redeem ourselves. Here in their towering home, we must learn to serve. To throw off the arrogance that took our wings and our starlight. We must submit ourselves to learn humility. Only then will we be taken up and returned to our former glory."

Everyone sighed, apparently imagining themselves with wings of light, flying around the clouds.

I nodded. "We're Lowforms to them now, but if we serve them with strength and honor, we'll someday get wings?"

Shari smiled. "Exactly. And now they've sent you here to us. You'll care for us and teach our babies. We'll send them out to serve the Hive. And one day, if you serve well, they'll come for you."

A banging sounded down the hall and a couple of the men jumped up. They disappeared down the corridor and returned carrying a huge vat of algae. Our circle broke up and everyone grabbed a woven bowl. Shari gave me one, and I lined up, following her lead. Everyone else seemed to know what to do, and I wanted to fit in as well as I could. We each dipped our bowls in the vat, filling them with the green slime. Once we all had our meals, we returned to the circle and sat, slurping our dinners. It was the same algae I was used to, and I hugged the bowl to my chest, needing something familiar to counter all the strangeness of my new life.

Shari continued her tale. "This is why we do it." She gestured around. "We're waiting. Waiting until we've truly learned the lessons our ancestors forgot. Waiting and serving until we're worthy to regain our wings. Those boys on the outside, hunting for food and keeping the Hive clean . . . they're working for all of us. Together we will show ourselves as the people we were meant to be. And sometimes one of us is taken up straight from here, like our mother was."

I licked the last of the slime from my bowl. It warmed me from the inside, and I sighed, resting back into my sister's arms.

"I don't remember our mother," I said.

"Of course you don't," Shari replied. "They come and take you very young. Start training you to help us all. But she was a wonderful woman. Full of love and kindness."

Glenna piped up from my other side. "Yes, she was a joy. We knew she'd be taken up one day."

"What's 'taken up' mean?"

Shari answered. "The Masters come and choose sometimes. It's always the oldest women and men, who have given full lives of service. They take them away from here, never to return. Outside, back to the place where we fell from the sky. The Masters lead them out, and proclaim them worthy. In the starlight, they are transformed. They shed this dirty shell, and their wings of glory unfold. They fly back into the night to live forever in service to the universe."

I had never seen this happen. In all my years in the Hive, I never saw anyone emerge from these halls into the upper chambers of the Hive. But surely they were right. I'd always known my life was meant to serve the Masters. I just never understood why.

Shari wrapped her arms around me from behind. "One day they will come for us all. We'll emerge into the light above, all together when they deem us all worthy of our wings. We'll follow each other up and up, and out under the sky. We'll walk to the place of our falling, and we'll receive our glorious wings. Until then, we'll wait here, serving the Hive."

The food in my belly made me sleepy, and a warm happiness filled my heart. Shari took me to an empty chamber and settled me down with a soft woven blanket. All the babies quieted and the toddlers stopped screaming.

"Good night, Chen," she said, and kissed me on the forehead.

I slept, and dreamed of the night sky.

CHAPTER 24

NOAH

I woke up in the bed where I had slept before. Warm furs were piled around me, and my mouth tasted like sour death. There was no way for me to tell what time of day it was. How long had I been asleep? How long had my Queen been without me?

Mo was there with a hot bowl of something that smelled warm and meaty. "You crazy fool," he said with a smile. "You got her. You really got her."

He put the bowl to my lips and I sucked at the strong broth. The flavor was nothing I'd ever had before, red and dark.

"Easy now." He took the bowl away. "Take your time. No good eating it if it's going to come right back up."

I reached out a hand and grabbed at the bowl. He let me have some more in little sips until I'd drained it.

"Where is she?" Her scent was everywhere and I wasn't awake enough at that moment to track it.

He chuckled. "She's fine. Happily sucking the life out of that seal, cuddled up with all the rest of them."

My heart twisted at that. I didn't want her on the seal. I was her chosen vessel. My body should be nourishing her. But as I pulled the furs off me, I could see that I had nothing to give her. The red, circular welt on my belly was caved in under sunken ribs. I would have died to feed her. The seal would. Did it feel what I felt? Did the bond of blood extend into the seal that now fed her? Was it filled with the glory of her presence, or terrified as its life drained away, second by second?

"Could we get more seals?"

Mo looked at me quizzically. "We can try to trap one. Are you still hungry?"

I shook my head. "Not for me. We don't eat them."

He looked at the empty bowl in my hands.

Oh.

"It's for the Queen," I said. "And for the other larvae. If we get more seals, they don't have to die. We could keep moving them from one to another, and let them go before they die."

Mo shrugged. "Maybe in the future we'll do that," he agreed. "The one down there is pretty used up, though. I don't think it would recover even if we pulled them all off right now."

I nodded. The Hive was bustling with the smells of newcomers, 'Mites drawn by her intoxicating scent. I didn't know them. And from what I knew of the people here, they wouldn't even realize if any of them meant her harm. I swung my legs off the pile of furs. The room swayed around me as I struggled to my feet.

Mo's arm grabbed under my shoulders and I leaned against him. "Steady, there. You've got a long way to go before you're full strength, son."

I stumbled forward. "Need to go see her." I looked down and realized I had no clothes on. The clothes I had left here were in a heap on the floor, and I pulled on the pants, wincing as the fabric slid over the rough scabs on my sides. "Need more food."

Mo helped me get dressed. "She's fine. I promise." He held the shirt, which billowed around my skinny form.

I had to rest a few moments after the exertion of dressing. Mo sat beside me.

"It was an incredibly brave thing you did, going to get her," he said. "Stupid, but brave." He pulled at the hairs on his arms as he spoke. "I know you have some kind of bond with her, and that's a good thing. But she's not just yours. She's the future for all of us. Every person and 'Mite in this Hive will protect her. When she grows up, she'll lead an army of her kind, and we'll be part of it. All those people, your friends still stuck in that Hive? We'll get them out once we're strong enough. Our people will never be slaves again. She's our Queen. All of us."

I nodded. Of course she would. She could do anything. My Queen would be the strongest in the world. And I would fight at her side to free my friends. We figured it would take a year before we were ready. The Queen would have to grow and molt into an adult, and our tiny band would have to grow, filled with 'Mites that would be loyal to her. Keeping her safe for all the months before our assault would take a lot of planning and moving. But Mo was sure that every move we made would draw more 'Mites to our cause. By the time our Queen was ready to lead us, we would have an army to fight.

The Hive was empty as I picked my way down the tunnels, guided by the scent of the Queen. *We need to do something about that,* I thought. *They're far across the mountains, but they'll smell her sooner or later.* I barely noticed the scent of 'Mites in the corridors over her beautiful blue smell.

When I got down to the incubation pool, it was alive with 'Mites. There was barely room to squeeze through them.

"How long have they been here?" I wondered.

Mo chuckled from behind me. "As soon as you arrived, they started showing up. Been coming in droves all day and night. There's thirty or forty now, mostly Diggers and the ones with the big jaws, but a couple of the Soldiers, too. It's a motley crew, but our army is growing every minute she's here."

They were a ragged lot. Something was wrong with each one of them . . . missing legs, broken claws. *Of course. They're outcasts from other Hives. Broken ones that are no good to their home Hive anymore.* Every one of them got my sniff test as I pushed my way through them. None smelled hostile. They were all just waiting. Hopeful. No aggression.

More would come every day. How could they not? And not a single one would get near her until I approved them.

I shoved through the last of them clustered around the pool. Hardly anything was left of the seal. The larvae had sucked it down to just skin stretched over bones. I flopped into the water next to it and laid my hand on the Queen. To my eyes, she looked the same as all the rest, only larger.

But to my nose and my touch, she looked like the brightest sunlight rippling on the ocean.

"I'm here," I whispered. "You're safe now."

I lay there for a while, my hand on her slick flesh. When I looked back at Mo, he was shaking his head.

"What do they do to you?" he muttered. "How do they make you slaves like that?"

My jaw clenched. "I'm not a slave."

He raised an eyebrow. "You're laying in the water next to a pile of maggots that are eating a half-dead seal. You're petting the fat one and whispering love songs to her. You almost died getting her here, and you screamed and clawed at us when we pulled her off you. You would have happily laid there and died just like that seal. So tell me you're not her slave."

"I'm not," I insisted. "A slave doesn't have a choice. A slave is owned. But I'm not owned. I choose to be hers. She's my Queen. I'm as much a part of her Hive as any of these 'Mites." I thought for a moment. "And they're not really hers. Not yet. Not like I am." I had shared her blood. The 'Mites around her were smitten with her scent, but only I was truly part of her glorious self. The roomful of giant insects clicked and whirred. Few of them would understand our language. Only ones from the sickly Yellow Hive where all my friends were captive.

Mo shrugged, looking just like his daughter in the gesture.

Where was she? I hardly smelled any humans in the Hive.

"Where did everybody go?" I asked him.

His face fell. "I sent them all away. We have a lot of

camps all over, places we go to stay away from the big Hive's soldiers. I sent almost everybody up into the mountains in case any of the 'Mites followed your trail here."

Of course they would. Without a direct trail to follow, it might take them a while to patrol out to where Sunshine had waited for me. But when they did, they'd track us straight here.

"We need to go," I said, popping up out of the water. "We need to go now."

He shook his head. "We can't leave them."

I followed his gaze to the larvae.

"But they'll be here. Probably not for a while yet, but they'll come."

Mo crouched next to me. 'Mites crowded around, over and under each other, each taking a turn to be nearest the Queen. "I know. But we can't take them. And we'll need them to take back the big Hive."

"No, we don't," I said. "We only need her. I'll take her back on my belly." *Where she belongs.* "As long as we keep her moist, it will be fine. You just keep feeding me and I can do it. I have strength enough for both of us."

Mo stared at me for a long moment. "Lexis has been studying these bugs her whole life. She thinks there's some kind of pheromone, some kind of bonding thing they do to keep the Hive together. How they act like one unit, and will happily die for the sake of the rest of them." He sighed. "Whatever they use, it's working on you, too."

"But not you?" How could he not feel it? She was right here.

"Nope." He ran a hand through his short gray hair. "And I don't want to risk your life feeding her, but you might be right." He looked around the crowded chamber. "If all these bugs found us already, the big Hive can't be far behind."

The Queen larva stirred. With a wet plop, she detached herself from the remains of the seal and flopped into the water. I reached for her, but she inched away from me. Using a hundred tiny appendages I hadn't realized she possessed, she crawled out of the pool. The 'Mites around us backed away, making a path in the direction she was traveling. She paused at the wall and reared back. Her tiny feet grabbed at the little imperfections, and she climbed. When she reached the ceiling, she stopped, hanging upside down by the hindmost feet.

As I watched with open mouth, she dangled there, wiggling. A thick, silky material oozed out of her head, and her movements propelled it all around her. Every head in the room was fixated on her progress. The scent of the silk was a warm, soft brown, like the beach at sunset.

Long moments passed. The silk flowed all around her until nothing could be seen of her inside it. As it dried from the top down, the shiny surface became dull and hard. The rest of the larvae followed her, dropping from the dead seal and creeping up the walls, spinning their own silken shells.

Finally it was finished. Eighteen hard cocoons hung from the ceiling of the chamber. All the 'Mites relaxed as one, and my shoulders lowered.

"It's time," I murmured. "Now we can only wait."

There was no moving those cocoons. I would have to be extra vigilant while my Queen transformed within it. She would rely on me to keep her safe from any threats while she was cemented to the ceiling, helpless and immobile.

"Blast it," Mo muttered. "We're not going anywhere

until that thing hatches."

As if I would leave her. As if I would ever stray from this room until my Queen emerged from her shell, a glorious adult ready to fight for all of us.

I smiled. "Can you bring my bedding down here? And some more food, please?"

Mo stalked away and I settled down on the hard ground underneath the cocoon to wait.

CHAPTER 25

KINNI

I shivered in the cold morning air and inched closer to the dying fire. Of all the camps we had all over the area, this high mountain cave was my least favorite. By far the safest since the cold kept the big bugs away, it was freezing and damp, it stank of bat poop, and the smoke from our fire hung in the air and choked my lungs. The smell of the cave mixed with the cloying scent from the floral wax candles we burned all around us to keep the smaller, biting insects from eating us alive in our sleep.

This was it.

This was my life.

When Dad and Lexis came up with their crazy plan to hatch a Queen bug that wouldn't be hostile to us, I thought he was crazy. I knew what those things could do.

I was only six years old when they raided the camp we

thought was safe. I had never seen them up close before. The land all around the big Hive was empty of the dangerous bugs, and the patrols from there had slacked off in the years since the Queen had conquered everything around. We got complacent.

Our camp was in a pine forest on the edge of a wide river, one of the few above-ground branches of the waterway that honeycombed under the whole area. The fields around it were thick with berry brambles and a tall, thin plant we could grind into flour and bake into flat bread on a hot rock. Mom was teaching me how to do it, pulverizing the little seeds in a stone bowl. There were all kinds of crustaceans in the rivers that cooked up sweet and juicy. Life was good.

The bugs attacked in the dark on a moonless night.

They were blind, and the darkness meant nothing to them. Their sense of smell and vibration was better than sight. We never had a chance.

Our population had grown a bit by then. We were almost up to a hundred people scratching out a living on a world ruled by insects. A lot of the women had multiple children by then as we started to feel safe enough to have them. My mom had just had twin boys, and I doted on my baby brothers.

We weren't totally stupid. We had sentries stationed all around our camp. They should have seen the bugs coming across the field. Should have cried out a warning. Only one of them managed to screech out a dying call as the soldiers overwhelmed them from all sides.

Everyone jumped up from where we slept under the low-hanging boughs. The darkness was chaos as bugs appeared from every side. People were screaming, but usually not for very long.

Someone grabbed me from behind and dragged me out toward the river.

"No! Mom and the boys!" I cried, but the arms kept pulling me away from the center of camp.

I saw them go down.

In the flickering light of fires from all around the camp, almost everything was a silhouette, but only my mom would have been carrying a baby under each arm. She was running from the massacre behind her. Men fought the bugs with the bladed weapons we made out of everything we could find on the planet. Some people had spears tipped with sharp metal, scrounged from the old wreckage of our ships during the pollen storms that kept the bugs away.

We thought those weapons would help us. But in the dark against an enemy that was taller and faster, that could "see" in pitch darkness and was armed with a venomous stinger, we were like mosquitoes fighting back against a colony of bats. Our blades rarely found their marks. Their stings rarely missed.

My mom ran through this chaos. Dad let go of me and raced toward her, shouting back at me as he went. "Get to the river! Swim downstream!" It was our escape plan from this camp: swim where the bugs couldn't follow and run when the river ducked underground.

Dad made it about three steps away. He thought I didn't see what happened, that he had been blocking my view, but I saw. One big soldier scuttled by. It didn't even turn a glance at my Mom, just swiped her with its tail in passing. The sting caught her in the back, and she pitched forward. Somehow she held onto my brothers as she fell.

Dad was still bolting towards her. He must have known he couldn't save her, but the boys . . . they were just babies. Their cries blended in with the screams of the night. Before he could get anywhere near them, another bug came and scooped them up, skittering back into the forest.

"Dad, no!" I screamed, and I don't know if he heard me, but he turned around and dashed back to where I was standing, frozen by the edge of the water. Without a backward glance he grabbed my arm and jumped with me into the river. We swam away from the carnage with the few survivors.

That was nine years ago. What did the bugs do with my baby brothers? Did they take them back to their huge, evil Hive and raise them as slaves like all the rest? Did they use them to incubate their horrible maggots? Did they eat them, or just leave them to die alone in the forest?

I huddled by the fire now, thinking back on that night, like I did every night when the fire burned low. The caves here were safer, but there was nothing to eat. We stockpiled as much as we could carry from the lowlands, but we couldn't live here forever. So we traveled, migrating in an ever-changing pattern, trying to stay one step ahead of the bugs that could destroy what was left of us on another dark night.

Dad's plan was crazy. But it might be our only chance. And that idiot had blown it.

I shook my head and burrowed deeper into my covers. The thick seal-hide wasn't soft, but piled on top of layers of woven silk, it was warm.

A figure burst into the cave mouth and we all jumped up, reaching for our weapons. My knife was in my hand before the seal-hide hit the ground.

But it wasn't a bug. It was Daniel, one of the men that had stayed behind with the larvae at the prairie Hive.

"He's back!" he said, and I looked around in confusion.

"He's back," Daniel repeated, stepping into the firelight. "He brought the Queen back. We're saved!"

CHAPTER 26

NOAH

I kept my vigil in the dark bowel of the crumbling Hive for days. More 'Mites kept arriving, drawn by the scent of our cocooned Queen. They all passed my smell test. No aggression. They smelled weary. Injured. But even through the cocoon, our Queen's scent gave them hope.

We were across the mountains from the Hive I'd escaped, and I hoped the Yellow Queen might be too old to bother with us, that her sickly Hive would just be content with the bounty they enjoyed at the hands of my friends. With each new 'Mite that showed up, my nerves grew more taut. Sooner or later, the Yellow Hive would come.

I didn't even know how long to expect the Queen and the rest to stay cocooned. Back at the Hive, we never saw this stage of the 'Mites' development. All we saw were the adults. Newly-hatched ones were smaller, but they grew and grew, molting their exoskeletons until they towered over us. A few of us saw the larvae, of course. I realized that now. But no one lived to tell the tale.

Back at the Hive, I'd always felt smart. I caught onto things quickly. Was one of the best at the clicking language of the 'Mites. I helped the younger boys with their tasks, and thought I was really something. Here, I was an idiot.

It wasn't just that I didn't know our history, where our people had come from. I didn't know anything. The first time I saw someone make a fire, I almost wet myself in terror as it flared up in front of him from sparks he made with rocks. There was no fire in the Hive. I never knew we needed it.

These people had weapons, slashing pieces of metal they'd pulled from the collapsing hulks of the ships in the Forbidden Zone. They had arrows, which they shot with bows strung with worm silk. They cooked their food and made marks on thin bark that other people could look at later and know what words it meant. And there were so many words I didn't know.

Mo taught me things over the next week. I was terrible at striking the fire rocks together, but my strong swimmer's shoulders made me pretty good with the bigger weapons. Mo said my Queen would lead an army of 'Mites to rescue our people and defeat the Yellow Queen. He said that we would fight along with them. I was a strong swimmer and a decent runner, but apart from some scuffles with other boys, I had never learned to fight, and we would never have been allowed to use weapons. Now I realized why. Hour after hour I practiced with the hard wooden spears and thick clubs, swinging at imaginary enemies in the dry dirt outside the Hive, trusting Sunshine to watch over the Queen in my absence. When the time came to fight, I would be ready.

I worked myself until my arms ached and my back cramped. A couple of the Builder 'Mites made large piles of the chewed clay and wood that made up Hive walls, and I bashed them down to dust. When I swung a club into a block of clay, my mind was full of the battle we would someday fight. So much better than the thoughts that plagued me when I wasn't smashing up targets.

But in the late afternoons when the heat stole my strength and I retreated to the cool depths near the pools, the questions burned in my brain. How had I never realized what we were in the Hive? How could I have lived my whole life in such blissful ignorance, happily serving a species that saw us as no more important than a seal in the river? I was at war with myself.

On one hand, I was completely devoted to the Queen in her cocoon. I would happily have died for her. The bond I felt was as much a part of me as an arm or leg. As more outcast 'Mites arrived from all over the area, I felt more and more possessive of her, and somehow more welcoming at the same time. We would all be her Hive together, reveling in her glorious blue scent, working together to ensure the health of the whole.

On the other hand, I knew what they were. I had learned the concept of slavery and realized what humans once were, and should have been. I still had little idea of the technology that had been taken from us in denying us access to our ships. The concept of interstellar distance was completely outside my ability to think. But those ships once flew. What must this place have looked like to those first humans who landed here? Through the red mist of pollen that gave them such a false security, what did they think of this land that became so hostile? When the 'Mites who became Masters swarmed over their ships, killing and enslaving almost all of them, did they hope for revenge? What would they think of me, bonded to one of their destroyers as I was?

And really, what was I?

Mo said one of their number had been taught some science, handed down from the original settlers. Her name was Lexis, and she had theories about the 'Mites and their scent markings. It was working on me, for certain. I belonged to the Queen. But was it real? Was my devotion to her a choice I was making, or just another form of chemical slavery?

"Noah, you okay?"

Mo startled me from my confused reverie.

I was sitting in the lower chamber where all of the cocoons hung from the ceiling, wanting to be there when the Queen emerged. 'Mites came and went, checking on her as I did. Surely she would remember me. Surely she felt the same about me as I did about her.

"Yeah, I'm okay. Just thinking."

He nodded. "It's so much to take in, isn't it?" There was a series of soft pops from his knees as he sat on the ground next to me. "But this is the start of something great. When that little Queen comes out, we're going to teach her everything we know. You're the best at that clicking language, and you'll teach her. She'll grow up here, nice and safe, and we'll just be part of the bug family. When we've got enough soldiers, we'll attack the big Hive and free the rest of our people. When we're all safe, we'll be able to do so much here. Farming and mining . . . The things we can build . . ."

I stiffened as a waft of pure terror shot through the tunnel.

Mo obviously didn't smell it, rattling on about how much better life would be.

I jumped up, along with every 'Mite in the place.

"What's wrong?" Mo unfolded next to me with more pops and creaks.

The smell of fear was all around me. 'Mites skittered around in olfactory panic.

I closed my eyes and breathed in. Rage coursed through me as the hated smell lanced into my head. The sickly yellow of the Hive where I was born. The aggression and venom of Soldiers in attack mode. And the devastating scent of death right above me.

"Stay with Queen," I clicked to the largest of the Diggers in the cavern with me. They formed a wall around the hanging cocoons, huge claws at the ready.

Mo was wide-eyed in confusion. He couldn't smell any of what was going on, but the sounds of battle echoed through the tunnels.

"They're here to kill her!" I shouted. "The Soldiers are here!"

CHAPTER 27

NOAH

I bolted up the long, curving tunnel. The sounds of fighting were everywhere, bouncing off the walls of the honeycomb of chambers all around me. My blood screamed to charge in and attack the invaders, but I gritted my teeth against the instinct, and turned toward my chamber instead. Without a weapon, I had no chance against a Soldier. I had to get a spear.

We had forty or fifty Outcasts in our ruined Hive that would fight to the death for our Queen. Mostly Diggers and Builders, but twelve were Soldiers, mostly missing legs and one missing its stinger. Four men, plus me.

And it smelled like at least ten Yellow Soldiers. Maybe more.

The spear was with the rest of the weapons in a little chamber they called an armory.

I raced into the room and ran smack into the back of someone.

He whirled around, eyes blazing.

Gil.

I backed a step away. "You're not dead? What are you doing here?"

His eyebrows met in a scowl of rage. "We're here to protect our Hive."

We. Our Hive.

In an instant I realized he didn't mean the free humans and our perfect Blue Queen. He meant the old Hive. The sickly Yellow Hive of death. He'd run straight back to them. And he'd led them straight back here.

I cocked back my shoulder and rammed a fist right into the side of his face. He crashed to the floor and didn't move.

"You really are an idiot," I muttered as I grabbed a spear and dashed toward the sounds and smells of the enemy.

It was impossible to count the number of invaders in the chaos of the battle. I closed my eyes and dashed into the fray, spear held high. The Yellows were advancing through our pathetic line, tails whipping left and right to sting our peaceful Diggers. Were they dead, or just paralyzed? It hardly mattered. If the invaders fought their way down to where the Queen hung in her cocoon, they would kill her.

Mo had instructed me not to throw the spear, but to jab with it. I saw two of the other men slashing with long metal knives, jumping and dodging the Yellow stingers. One of their Soldiers went down under a pile of Diggers, and the smell as they ripped it to shreds with their huge claws made my heart sing.

We can do this. We can win.

Out of the corner of my eye, I saw three of the Yellow Soldiers dash from the fray and skitter toward the lower tunnels, heading for the Queen. I bolted after them.

Down they went, following the scent trails we left as we traversed the deep tunnels. They were faster than I was. They were going to get to her.

From out of a side tunnel, two Builders bowled into the Soldiers. One was stung instantly and fell, partially blocking the tunnel. As the Soldiers climbed over its still body, the other Builder hunkered down right in front of them.

The Builder's head exploded.

In an instant the tunnel was filled with a noxious, choking gas. The stench invaded right into my brain, stopping me cold. I was blind. I couldn't smell a thing.

The Soldiers were also blinded, and in that moment, I realized the advantage was mine.

I couldn't smell, but I could see.

With primal scream, I flung myself onto the back of the Soldier in the rear. I buried my spear into the back of its neck, and it dropped beneath me. I wrenched out the spear, rolled away from the still-dangerous tail, and scrambled to my feet.

The other two Soldiers heard me. They couldn't navigate well, but their feelers could surely detect my motion. One of them advanced on me.

And the other turned and resumed a much slower march down the tunnel, touching the wall to stay on course.

It's going for her. Stop it.

But an enraged Soldier stood between me and my quarry.

It whipped its stinger around wildly, searching for me in its blindness. I dodged left, but the thick tail whizzed toward me. With another yell, I plunged the tip of my spear into the meat of the tail. It stuck there, and the strength of the Soldier ripped the haft right out of my hands. The spear clattered away as the noxious explosion smell was replaced by a stronger acid stench.

I feinted to the right, hoping to dash past it and run to defend the Queen in the lower chambers.

But the tail hit me square in the left thigh.

Numbness washed over my leg. I lunged toward the fallen Builder, hoping to crawl under its still bulk before total paralysis hit me.

The stinger hit me again, this time in the right leg. But the numbness didn't come. I couldn't feel anything on my left side below the hip, but the paralysis stopped there.

Another wave of the acid stench scorched my nostrils.

My spear. It ruptured the venom sac.

The Soldier was out of venom.

I groped for my fallen spear and my hands closed around something sharp. In the dim light I could barely tell what it was, but the stench told me where it came from. I was holding the huge, serrated mandible of the Builder that had somehow exploded its own head to save us.

With a feral roar, I flung myself at the Soldier. My movement was awkward, swinging my dead leg around, but the Soldier was still disoriented by all the conflicting smells in the narrow tunnel. The mandible in my hand was heavier and sharper than any of the weapons the humans here had made. I lunged right into the Soldier's waving front legs. It closed them around me and plunged its useless tail into me again.

I swung the mandible in my hand, putting all the power

of rage and terror into the swing.

The Soldier's head flew from its thorax and splatted into the wall. We fell together into a pile of limbs and gore.

CHAPTER 28

NOAH

There was no time to bask in my triumph. The farther the last enemy Soldier got from the fumes here, the faster it would run toward our helpless Queen.

Blood soaked through my pants from each of the stinger holes. My left leg was still dead weight, but I hauled myself up, climbing on the body of the Soldier. I crawled over and retrieved my spear, clambering over the dead 'Mites blocking the tunnel. On the other side, I leaned against the left wall and swung my dead leg forward. Using my spear to support my weight, I limped forward, down toward the sound and smell of battle.

In the Queen's chamber, Mo and two Diggers were backed up into the pool where the larvae had incubated. Three other Diggers lay unmoving in the water; dead or paralyzed, I couldn't tell.

The Diggers waved their huge claws, snapping at the Soldier.

With a flash of the tail, the enemy stung one of the Diggers. It collapsed into a heap.

The other jumped onto the Soldier and plunged its claw right into the venomous tail. The Soldier flung itself to the side, and the Digger flew off and crashed into the wall. Its claw remained embedded in the Soldier's tail and the air filled with the acid smell of venom.

That's it. We've won.

Mo leaped at the Soldier. It crouched down and took the force of the unarmed man onto its hard shell. The tail whipped around and punctured Mo before swishing him off into the pool. Without the venom, the sting wouldn't be fatal, but Mo was old. He reached up from the water as the Soldier skittered past, but couldn't rise to follow.

The Soldier raced for the cocoons. The Queen's was in the back, protected by the others that had woven their shells all around her.

Soldiers didn't have huge, strong claws on their forearms like Diggers, but they had plenty of strength in the small, sharp pincers. It ripped at the first of the cocoons, pulling it open and spilling the liquid contents onto the hard floor.

The smell electrified me. But I was so far away. And with my dead leg, I couldn't run.

Another cocoon crashed to the floor.

I raised my arm and cocked it back.

The spear flew from my hand and buried itself into the Soldier's back.

It grabbed at one last cocoon as it fell, pulling the shell down to the ground.

I dropped to the floor and crawled as fast as I could, clutching the sharp mandible in my hand. Mo reached out for me as I slithered past, but I did not stop.

Through a puddle of leaking venom I crawled, and dragged myself up onto the body of the dying Soldier.

My mandible made short work of it, and as its head popped from its body, I looked up to the ceiling where my Queen's cocoon hung, white and unharmed.

"We did it. We saved you."

I collapsed on top of the dead enemy and the room went black.

When the battle was over, we had lost two-thirds of our 'Mites. One of the men, a quiet, olive-skinned guy named Sean, was dead. Mo was bruised and torn, but would recover. My puncture wounds oozed blood, but in a matter of hours a painful tingling in my left foot told me the venom was wearing off. I would walk again. Mo wondered if my previous stings back in the Hive had given me some immunity to the venom. If so, it probably saved my life.

Our army was a disaster. The 'Mites that remained were even more battered than before. More missing limbs. More scars. Sunshine survived the battle intact, and clicked sadly over the bodies of the dead.

But we had done it. We had defended her.

Those of us that remained gathered in the main chamber near the entrance. The surviving Diggers were dragging out bodies, but the stench still permeated the hall.

Mo and I sat together, with the other three men and all

the 'Mites around us. Gil sat in the corner, guarded by two Builders. His right eye was already turning blue and swollen mostly shut.

I shook my head, looking at him. "Why would he do that? Go back when he knew they'd kill him?"

He muttered from the corner, "They weren't. I was gonna be a hero."

My leg screamed as I jumped to my feet and limped over to him. "A hero? You really are an idiot. They were never going to let you live out this day. They came to kill our Queen, and then you'd be worthless."

His voice was nasal, probably from the swelling. *Good.* "They were gonna make me head of all the Lowforms."

I snorted. "Humans. Slave humans. Not Lowforms. Don't ever call our people that. And if you believed them, you're stupider than I thought." I turned back to Mo. "Kinni said you had tried to rescue some of us before, and they always went running back. Who were they? What were their names?"

He thought for a moment. "Micah was the last one. I think . . . Cody before that."

I remembered both of them. Runners, a few years older than me. They both disappeared, like Runners so often did.

"Micah and Cody," I said, crouching next to Gil. He flinched back away from me. *Good.* "Both of them brought here. Both of them ran back to our Hive. You ever see either one of them again?"

Gil shook his head, wincing.

"Of course not. As soon as the Soldiers saw them, they had to kill them. Couldn't let them bring the truth back to a Hive full of slaves." I sighed. "They'd have killed you right here, and you know it."

He didn't answer, just glared at me with his one good eye.

I turned back to the room. "We have to get reinforcements," I said. "They'll be back."

Carl, one of the other men, grinned, wrapping a bandage around a long cut on his arm. "Those ones won't."

"No," Mo said, "Noah's right. When this patrol doesn't come back, they'll send another. They'll follow the scent trail these soldiers left. More of them, most likely."

I nodded. "Who knows how many? And it won't be long."

We looked around the room. Fourteen injured 'Mites, and five humans, including me. That was all our defense.

"That was pretty smart, using that jawbone as a weapon," Mo said to me with a smile. He turned to the other men. "You guys should have seen it. He was a madman. Just flung himself on that bug and cut its head clean off."

Warmth spread over my face. "Didn't have much choice." I turned to the Builder nearest me and switched from the human language to the clicking 'Mite language. I didn't have words for what I wanted to say, so I clicked, "Head. Smell. Gone," and pantomimed a head exploding.

It clicked assent. "Yes. Save Queen."

The other guys were looking quizzically at us and I explained. "We were fighting in the hallway and one of the Builders just hunkered down and blew its own head off. Just . . . made it explode somehow. The stench was unbelievable. Even you guys would have been sick." They all knew that my sense of smell had been changed, heightened to 'Mite level, or nearly so. No one seemed to know how contact with the

Queen larva had done it, but it hardly mattered.

"So," Mo said. "What do we have now?" He looked around the room and sighed. "We have to hold on here until the Queen hatches. Once she does, we can clear out of here and find somewhere safer until she grows up."

I shook my head. "They'll smell her for miles. We'll get more outcasts, for sure, but the Hive will send everything they have now that they know she's here." I shot a glare at Gil. "How long does it take for a Queen to become adult?"

Clicking from the 'Mites indicated six months.

"No way." I rubbed at my leg, still tingly from the venom. "We have to get far from here. Miles and miles. Farther than anyone has ever traveled."

Mo shrugged. "And who's to say we won't run into another Hive that wants to kill her? We can't take her up to the mountains. It's too cold. She'd never survive."

Carl tied off the bandage on his arm. "So . . . what then? We just wait here until they send more bugs to kill us all?" He spit on the ground. "Doesn't matter anyway, really. Without the rest of the people they got in that Hive, there's not enough of us to last another generation. Might as well die here."

Mo opened his mouth to retort, but I silenced them all with a wave of my hand, my eyes closed in sudden rapture.

The sweetest scent billowed up from below. Ice blue, like the shallows of the sea on a calm day.

"She's emerged. Our Queen is here."

CHAPTER 29

KINNI

Lexis was smarter than any of us. She was always mixing things up, working from a bunch of handwritten notes in a faded notebook. She said that in the early days of our peoples' flight, they had access to a world of knowledge on some kind of device. They knew the devices wouldn't last long without repairs, so they tried to write down anything they thought might help them survive in this hostile country.

There was a lot of stuff about bugs.

It's how we knew that our 'Mites were a lot like tiny insects that built giant mounds back on Earth. No way Earth people would have ever believed ours, though.

The book had all kinds of things about growing plants, treating injuries, making weapons. A lot of it didn't apply here, because the plants were all different, but over the years our people had sorted a lot of things out.

None of it seemed to be helping much.

I was wrapping cord around an arrowhead, attaching it to a thin shaft of hardened reed, when I heard the boom. It sounded like a crack of thunder, and the whole cave shook. The air filled with the sound of a thousand bats flapping frantically around the part of the cave they roosted in.

Sunlight streamed through the open doorway. *So . . . not thunder.* I set down the arrow and followed a crowd of people outside to see what had made the noise.

Lexis was standing with her back to us, peering into a hole in the ground that I was sure hadn't been there the night before. It was about an arm's length across, and the edges of it were black. When Lexis turned around, her face was covered in soot. Under the grime, it looked like her eyebrows might not be there.

"It works!" She was grinning, teeth white against her filthy lips. "I did it!"

All the bats chose that moment to fly out of the cave. We all ducked as the dark cloud streamed by.

People crowded around the hole. I sidled in and looked over the edge, but nothing was down there. Just more black rock.

"What did you do?" I asked.

Lexis beamed. She pulled the old notebook out from under the back of her shirt. "I made an explosive."

People backed away from the hole, eyeing it with suspicion. Nobody seemed to want to know any more about it, and after a moment, Lexis's face fell.

She looked so disappointed that nobody had any questions, so I glanced at the book she was waving around. "How did you do it?"

The old, dry pages rustled as she opened the book and pointed to a scribbled note. "See? It's bat guano. What you do is, you soak it in water for a couple of days. Then you filter out the crystals, and you mix them with sulfur." She pointed up the mountain. "This was a volcano at one time, eons ago. There's sulfur all around the rim. Took me all day to climb up and get some."

I looked up the hill but the rocks looked the same as all the others around here. Dead and dry.

"So then," she continued, "you take the crystals and the sulfur and you mix it with charcoal." Her eyes turned serious. "And then you're very, very careful with it."

"Why?" I asked.

"Because it explodes," she said. "It's not very stable, and super flammable. Just one little spark, and boom!"

I peered back into the black hole at her feet. "Boom, for sure. How much of that stuff did you make?"

She glanced over at a couple of bowls sitting on the far side of the plateau. "Just a handful. I can make more." She grinned at the cave opening. "Not like we have a shortage of bat poop."

I hadn't known what "guano" meant. Now I did, and wished I didn't. Exploding bat poop. Just what we needed.

"Could you make enough to blow up the big Hive?"

She nodded. "Probably. I wouldn't want to transport that much. And we don't want to kill our people inside."

Well, no. But if we could get our people out . . . not that I had any idea how we'd do that.

"But we could maybe figure out how to stabilize it. Turn it into some kind of weapon we could use. Find some safer place to live and rig some kind of barrier so the bugs can't get in."

I didn't mention that if they couldn't get in, we probably couldn't get out. It would take an awfully big perimeter to cordon off an area big enough to support even the small number of people we had left. Maybe if our territory included a river where we could trap seals . . .

No reason to put a damper on her mood, though. "That's amazing," I said, faking a huge smile. "Maybe this is a turning point for us."

She grinned and turned back to the notebook, making her own notes in the margins. "Maybe if the Queen that Noah brought back survives, we might just have a shot. This could give us the advantage in a fight. Finally."

We hadn't heard anything more from the people we left with the larvae. My dad was down there. He'd told us not to come down until they sent a runner up to get us, and if we didn't hear from them by next pollen storm, to move on to the next camp, farther down the hill on the other side. It wasn't as safe as up there, but there were a lot of fruit trees and berry bushes we could harvest before moving to the camp after that. The endless cycle of trying to stay one step ahead of the giant bugs that wanted to kill us all.

CHAPTER 30

NOAH

She was beautiful.

By the time I jumped to my feet, recognizing the scent of our newly emerged Queen, the corridors had filled with 'Mites streaming in from outside. I pushed and shoved but couldn't get past them. We flowed down the long tunnels as one, with the humans bringing up the rear.

The pool chamber was filled with 'Mites when I elbowed my way in. All our misfit fighters clustered around a vision of perfection, perched on the ground below her shattered cocoon.

She was no taller than my chest. Her eight legs were delicate, still damp and shining from the inside of her cocoon. They joined her body in a star shape at her thorax. Her small head glistened in the light of the torches, and her tail was longer than my whole body. She sat back on her hind six feet, waving the front two at us all. Her feelers tasted the air around her.

Other 'Mites were emerging from their own shells, dropping to the floor behind her. They waved their legs around, drying off.

I pushed my way through the mass of adults to the front of the group surrounding her. As soon as she smelled me, she whipped her head around and stretched her front legs toward me.

"I'm here," I murmured, and stepped toward her. Her scent was intoxicating, and I had a hard time keeping my footing.

When I reached her, she touched my shoulders with her forelegs. Her feelers tasted my face, tickling my skin. I reveled in her touch.

"You remember me?" Did I dare to hope?

Her forelegs wrapped around me and pulled me in. She dropped her head and I reached up to touch her shining skin. A pale yellow oil oozed out of the top of her head and I wiped it away.

The instant I touched the oil, my world went fuzzy. A shiver of pure joy rushed through me. It was like when she had been attached to me, but so much more. My lungs pumped, sucking in the scent of the sweet oil on my fingers.

"I'm yours forever," I whispered.

It was all there. The Hive bond. I had been hers from the mingling of our blood back at the old Hive. I would have given her every drop I had. This was her response. I was hers, and she was mine. I felt it with every breath. I would die for her. And she would live for me.

She released her hold on me and I stepped back, lost

in the awe of the moment. One of the adult 'Mites gently pulled me back and took my place in front of the Queen.

She pulled the 'Mite in and it rubbed its head against hers, tasting the sweet oil. When it stepped back, I wanted to embrace it.

I had no words for what I felt for that 'Mite. Brother wasn't strong enough. It shared the favor of my Queen. I should have been jealous, but her power was strong enough to surround us all. One by one the adult 'Mites approached her and received the oil. When each one backed away, it joined the group of us all together, milling around the room, sharing the rapture of the moment. One Hive. One family. Glory to our Queen.

"What in all the hells is going on?"

Even Mo's voice couldn't disrupt my joy.

"We're hers," I tried to explain. "We're a real Hive now. She's our Queen, and we're her 'Mites."

"You're not a 'Mite," he pointed out, and I grinned.

"I am, though. I am now."

The newly hatched came next, accepting her blessing. They shivered with the same obvious joy I felt.

"Go," I urged Mo. "She's Queen of us all. Go and touch her and you'll see."

He raised an eyebrow at me. The other men eyed me like I'd grown an extra head.

Mo frowned. "I'm not sure I want to. We're free here."

I knew what he meant. I remembered what it was like to be on the outside, seeing the bond of a Hive but not able to be part of it, or even to understand what that meant. As a kid I'd wanted nothing more than to serve my Masters. But this was different.

"It's not like that," I said. "I'm still free." I glanced back at the Queen, giving her oil to all our 'Mites. "I'm not her slave. I'm her family."

Mo hesitated a moment, then his jaw clenched as he made up his mind.

He approached the Queen. She took a step back, tasting him with her feelers. After a long moment, she lowered her head and he rubbed his hands in the oil she secreted.

He waited.

He turned around to face me.

"So what's supposed to happen? Shouldn't I feel something?"

I was too blissed out to register more than a faint disappointment. "Maybe it's only for me. Because she was attached to me. Maybe you can't really be hers."

A gargled scream echoed behind me. It cut through my hazy joy and sent a chill down my back.

Gil barreled through the 'Mites that stood there enjoying the Queen's blessing. He crossed the room at a dead run, arms raised.

He's going to hurt her.

My feet felt like lead. Gil lunged at the Queen, who skittered back out of his reach. He stumbled over the edge of the pool, splashing into the water.

Go. Help her. Protect the Queen. The scent of it filled the room, the Queen's blue tinged with silver, icy fear.

The nearest 'Mites jumped on Gil, dragging him away from the Queen. I grabbed at his flailing arms, pulling him out of their grasp. Raw fury oozed out of them, and crawled through my veins. We wanted to tear him apart.

"No! Noah, don't!" Mo pulled Gil from my grasp and

shoved him away. The 'Mites formed a protective circle around the Queen, every feeler aimed straight at Gil. The few Soldiers that had survived the battle raised their venomous tails toward him.

I saw the moment it happened.

His face was a mask of pure hatred, staring murderous rage at the small Queen behind her guards. But in seconds, his expression melted into confusion. He rubbed at his arm where I'd grabbed him. The slick of oil that had been on my hands glistened on his skin.

He brought his fingers to his face and inhaled deeply.

Gil crumbled in front of us all.

He collapsed, sobbing, rubbing his face with his hands.

I strode toward him and stood over his weeping form.

His voice was a harsh rasp, and when he looked up, I knew.

"My Queen," he whispered. "I'm so sorry, my beautiful Queen."

CHAPTER 31

NOAH

We all gathered in the main hall. The young 'Mites and Queen were surrounded by the adults. Five more refugee 'Mites had arrived since the battle, waiting outside until I allowed them entry. None of our Hive would mistake them for enemies, but the Queen's safety depended on vigilance. No 'Mite approached to receive her oil without my initial okay. And no other 'Mites even considered questioning the authority I'd taken on in this task. Even our strongest Soldiers deferred to me when I stalked through the Hive to sniff out a stranger. Mo might be in charge of the human population, but I was in charge of the Hive.

To ease my muscles after the fight, I'd made a long dive into the underground river here and harvested a basket of waterbugs, which the 'Mites were enjoying raw. I was famished, and ate three of my own. The other men wrinkled their noses.

"Those look disgusting. How can you eat that?" They munched on dry strips of seal.

I grinned. "It's the best. How can you eat THAT?"

Mo sat down next to me, chewing on his meat strip, eyeing my raw waterbug. "Those have got to be so full of parasites . . . Is that what they fed you?"

The shell of the last waterbug cracked in my hands and I slurped it down. "These, and the other shellfish, and the algae from the ship, I guess. Whatever else the Gardeners could grow in the mushroom patches or gather from the land around."

He shook his head at my slimy meal. "So what happened down there?"

"It's . . . I don't know how to describe it." The 'Mites had tried to tell me, but the clicking language didn't have words for what they did. "It's a thing for them. I saw it back at the old Hive, on that last day when the old Queen laid her eggs on me. They all did just what we did. Got that oil from their Queen." I shivered in disgust. She was ancient. Sick. Her oil would be foul and putrid. "It's a thing they do, apparently. All the Hive goes down to get the oil. It's . . ." I trailed off. How could I express the pure rapture that coursed through me when I received her blessing? Mo had tried and felt nothing.

"But it didn't work for me," he said. "I touched it and felt nothing. Still got nothing."

"No. I don't know why. Maybe because she shared my blood?"

He glanced at Gil, who was fawning over the Queen in the corner. All the 'Mites had accepted him. His whole scent had changed. "But it worked on Gil, apparently. He touched that stuff and got . . . what, converted? Inducted?"

"She made him hers." I sucked down the last waterbug and licked out the shell. "I don't understand it. But her oil made him part of the Hive. We all are." I gestured around the room. "It's like . . . like all of us are just part of the same body, different parts of one big thing." I wished I had words for what I wanted to express, but they didn't exist.

"He didn't share her blood, though," Mo said. "She was never on him, was she?"

"No."

"So why does it work on him and not on us?"

I had no answer.

Mo stood up and stretched. "Well, maybe Lexis can figure it out." He looked around the room. "We need to let them all know what's happened here. The attack, and the Queen. We need to get everyone together and sort out a plan."

Exhaustion was tugging at my bones. The wounds I'd taken in the battle that morning felt hot, and every muscle ached.

"We should be safe for a couple of days at least," I said. "The old Hive won't expect their Soldiers back right away, and when they don't return, they'll have to sort out another patrol to send at us."

The Queen in the corner folded her legs under her and lowered her head. All the young ones clustered around her, and the adults settled in, guarding the sleepy juveniles.

"But they'll smell her for miles," I continued. "We need to get our people out of there and get far away from here. They won't stop. They can't."

Gil wandered over and plopped down next to me. "They'll never stop until she's dead," he agreed. "I can't explain it. I wasn't even thinking, just had this impossible need to kill her. Until she accepted me as hers."

Mo shook his head. "I don't get it. And right now, I'm too tired to think." He set up a night watch rotation among the humans, knowing the 'Mites would set their own. "In the morning we'll send a runner up the mountain. See what we can come up with. And now, I'm going to bed."

He stalked away to his chamber.

I pulled my pile of hides out and snuggled up to sleep next to the Queen.

In the morning, we started harvesting what we could from our dead 'Mites. The huge Digger claws that cut right through rock could be mounted onto a handle and swung like a sword. I'd proven that Builder mandibles were formidable. It felt wrong to be taking these parts from 'Mites who had died to save our new little Hive, but I knew that if I had died and some part of me could be used to keep the Queen safe, I'd want the survivors to take it and use it.

And it was obvious that we would need weapons, and practice using them. Soldier 'Mites were born to kill. We had a lot of catching up to do.

The men argued about where to go as we all harvested the sharp parts from the dead 'Mites.

Carl thought we should take all the 'Mites up to the cave where the rest of our people were currently hiding. "We can build enough fires and keep them inside close by. They'll stay warm enough."

"And what will they eat?" Mo crouched next to a dead Digger, using a mandible to saw the claw into two usable parts. "What will we eat? You know there's nothing up there."

"So what's your plan?"

Mo's shoulders sagged. "I don't have one." He looked over to where I was working on another unfortunate Builder. This one had been missing a leg when it showed up. It was missing more than that now. "I didn't think they'd be able to find us here. Thought once we got her, we'd have time to raise her before we attacked the Hive to get our people back."

I pulled at the strong jaw on the dead 'Mite. "They'll never leave us alone here. What's the other way?" I pointed away from the coast where the sick Hive was, toward the long flatlands and low hills I'd never known existed.

"More 'Mites," Carl said. "A million smaller Hives, all stinking mad as soon as they see you."

Mo nodded. "The Queen on the coast, the one that has our people, she's lived a long time. Way too long. Should have been replaced by new Queens. But having our people to do all their work made her way too powerful. No other Hives anywhere around; she killed them all. But when you leave her territory, they're everywhere, all battling among themselves. There's nowhere safe."

I sat back on the ground in the sunshine. The sky was grayer today than usual. Mo had told me the whole planet was surrounded by a cloud of tiny rocks flying in space. The sky didn't look like rocks. Just like a high, gray cloud, some days thick and dark, others open to distant blue.

"Then what are we waiting for?"

They looked at me.

"They're going to keep coming. We know that. We're not going to be safe as long as she rules that Hive. So let's figure out a way to get our people out of there and kill the Hive once and for all."

CHAPTER 32

NOAH

The rest of the people came back late that night, trooping down from whatever mountain hideaway they'd been staying in. Lexis started directing the Builders and Diggers to start fortifying our Hive, with plans for a wall and a trench around it. Her eyebrows were missing, but I didn't want to ask.

All day long there had been a steady trickle of new outcasts. Our Queen seemed to enjoy sitting in the sunshine, welcoming each 'Mite with her oil. I sniffed them out as they arrived, but the Queen's serene glow kept the edge off my nerves. Our numbers were growing, but nowhere near enough. Hardly any of the outcasts were Soldiers, and the few that were had obvious physical issues. Some army.

Lexis had a million questions for me.

"So you said that the Builders and Diggers at the old Hive helped you escape?"

I sat back on the ground, securing a Builder mandible
to a thick wooden club. I thought back to my flight, with
the Queen attached to my belly. "It sure seemed like it. They
could smell her for sure."

"But the Soldiers attacked?"

The memory of angry Soldiers raining down into the
water sent a chill down my back. "They sure did."

"Why?"

I had no answer for that. We had allies within the old
Hive. 'Mites of every class that realized their old Queen was
sick. Her weakness was poisoning the whole Hive. Those few
allies had orchestrated our escape in the first place. Did I just
get lucky, and happen to run into more allies who recognized
what we were doing?

"I don't know," I said. "Maybe because they're inside
with the Queen all the time, the Builders and Diggers are
feeling the sickness more? Maybe they're more accepting of
a new one?"

A clicking sounded behind me. I turned to see a Soldier
outcast, one of the few that had survived our battle. "Builders
stupid," it clicked. "No Hive-is-us." It meant loyalty, but
there was no word for that in the click language. "Follow
any Queen."

Lexis smiled. "That makes sense. With some Earth
insects, a new Queen would leave her old Hive with some of
the workers and set up a new one somewhere else. Probably
with these bugs, some of the worker classes would follow
the new Queen and be there to build a new Hive around
her. Insect behavior, and insect larval stage with molting
on an eight-legged monster that's technically an arachnid. I
wouldn't have expected it, but here we are."

She was also full of questions about the oil sharing, which she called a ritual. The Queen had favored her with oil, but like Mo, it didn't change her scent. She didn't bond. Wasn't "us."

"Gotta be some reason it works on you," she said, pointing a Digger where she wanted it to work. "We're all the same people, genetically. Doesn't make sense that you'd get it and we wouldn't. But we'll keep trying. Maybe we have to do it more than once because we haven't been around them as much." She eyed one of the younger guys who was sawing the claw off one of our dead Diggers. "Maybe Mo and I are too old for it to work. Who knows?" She was making a list of every difference she could come up with, and theorized that there was something in the old Hive that changed our brain chemistry so we were susceptible.

Later that night, we all crowded together in the common room. We had maybe thirty-five people, and thirty 'Mites. I was using a bit of Builder mandible to cut a dead 'Mite's thick back armor into small, sharp arrowheads.

Mo sat at the front of the group, and in the back, Gil clicked a translation for the 'Mites of my old Hive that understood the clicking language. Our new Queen was learning fast, and her feelers waved, tasting all the scents of the room.

"So what do we know, and what do we have?" Mo said.

Lexis sighed. "We've got decent weapons, but nothing that will take down a Hive full of Soldiers. I've been working on an explosive, but I can't blow up the enemy Hive with our people still in it. We're not safe here, but we're not safe anywhere that the 'Mites can go with us. And we'll need them if we're ever going to rescue our people."

Carl muttered from my left. "We need more Soldiers. All these Diggers are great, but in a fight, we need venom."

I looked at the arrowhead I was working on and thought about the acid smell when I had stabbed the enemy Soldier's tail. "Could we maybe take the poison from the dead ones?"

Everyone stared at me and I swallowed, suddenly hot. "I mean, they've got, like, a bag of it in their tails, right? Could we get it out and use it? Make some kind of weapon for ourselves?"

A murmur went around the room.

Lexis tapped a fingernail against her teeth in thought. "Noah, ask the Soldiers if they can squeeze it out at will, or if it just happens when they sting something."

I clicked out the message as best I could. In response, the nearest Soldier raised its tail. In a moment, a drop of acid appeared on the tip of its stinger.

A grin made Lexis stop tapping. "Oh, that's good. So we milk the Soldiers we do have, and coat our arrows and spears with their neurotoxin. That could change things a lot in a straight fight."

"A straight fight is not remotely what we want," Mo said, and all the humans nodded.

"No," Lexis said, tapping again. "But if we could get all the Soldiers out of the Hive somehow, and get our people out, then next pollen storm when they're all inside, I could try and blow their Hive up with them inside it."

She'd explained about her explosive. I was still quite hesitant about the whole concept of fire, and couldn't really imagine what she was talking about.

"Problem is," Carl said, "if we get all the Soldiers out, they'll kill every one of us. Even with poison arrows, we're nowhere near enough in a fair fight."

Kinni piped up from the back of the room. "You just said it, though, didn't you?" We all swiveled to look at her. She grinned and pointed at me. "He knows how to do it. And we're not fighting fair."

CHAPTER 33

NOAH

At the end of the night, we all lined up for our evening ritual. Several new 'Mites had arrived that day and awaited the Queen's blessing. She stood up tall at the front of our main chamber, and the new 'Mites lined up to bond with her. One by one they approached, and she favored them with her oil. The scent of it sent shivers of joy up my back, and Lexis stood back, shaking her head as the newly-anointed 'Mites collapsed to the ground, shaking with ecstasy.

Lexis tried again, wiping the oil from the Queen's gland onto her hands. She sniffed it, rubbing it between her fingers. She licked it and made a gagging face.

"Not tonight, evidently."

Her gaze traveled over the group.

"Everybody needs to try it. I need to understand how this works. Like it or not, we can't live without a Hive."

The humans grumbled, and I looked to the Queen to see her reaction. The oil was not Lexis's to give. But the Queen waved her feelers in the air, and her scent was sky blue, serene and content.

Lexis lined everyone up. I slipped in behind Kinni, always eager to get another dose for myself.

One by one, the people approached the Queen. Most tentatively reached out one finger, dabbing it on her head. They smelled of fear and anxiety. *They don't want it to work. They're afraid of turning into mindless slaves.* But Gil and I weren't mindless. I wished I could help them understand. I hadn't lost myself in the Queen. I had found myself in the Queen.

"Smell it. Everybody take a good whiff." Lexis watched each one in turn.

I worried that the Queen would run out of oil or patience, but her scent never changed. She loved us so much, even those of us who couldn't sense her happy blue waves. There was no way she could possibly understand the danger she was in. But she knew that humans and 'Mites had already died for her. She knew we would do it again.

Kinni stood in front of her.

"This is so gross. Do I have to do this?"

A look from Lexis convinced her that she did. "We need to understand this. There's got to be a reason it's not working here."

Kinni took a deep breath and reached out one hand. The Queen leaned into her touch, and Kinni's hand came away damp with oil.

"Anything?"

Kinni shook her head. "Nope."

I went next, reveling in the bond.

"Kinni?" Behind me, Lexis's voice was concerned.

By the time I turned around, Mo was catching Kinni as she fell to the floor of the chamber. Her eyes were rolled back in her head, and she held the oil-soaked hand to her face.

"Kinni, are you okay?" Lexis pushed her way over to Kinni and Mo. "Kinni? Are you sick?"

A tremor shot through Kinni's arms and legs, and Mo held her close to his chest. He turned an angry eye to me.

"What's happening to her? Have you ever seen this happen?"

I stared, breathing deep.

Kinni. Welcome.

In a few seconds, Kinni's face cleared. She looked up at the Queen with wonder in her eyes.

Her dad held her face in both of her hands. "What is it? Are you all right?"

Kinni smiled at the Queen, pulling air in through her mouth and nose. She nodded, not yet capable of making words.

"She's one of us. It worked."

I crouched down next to her and Mo let me take Kinni's limp hand.

"What do you mean, 'she's one of us?'"

Her scent was changing with every breath I took. Humans smelled warm and sticky, not an unpleasant odor, but not clean like a 'Mite. Kinni still smelled human. But every time she exhaled, I got a brighter glow from her breath.

I looked at Mo and grinned. "She's part of the Hive now. She belongs to the Queen."

Kinni's rapt expression was broken by the flaring of her

nostrils. "You're still an idiot," she whispered. "But you're my idiot." She looked back to the Queen. "And I'm hers."

CHAPTER 34

NOAH

The air was red with pollen. A million tiny plants that grew over every surface released the tiny particles every month, all at once. It gritted in my eyes and destroyed my sense of smell entirely. Unlike the 'Mites that followed us tentatively through the hills, I had eyes to see, but the sense I had come to depend on was completely blind.

We had left the Queen and Soldiers hunkered down in our little Hive, along with a few of our people. They were safe from attack as long as the wind blew red. Even if the old Hive realized where we were and what we had done to their initial attack, they couldn't follow the trail until the storm stopped without a human who knew the way to guide them. We had three days to work. The remainder of the humans had returned up the mountain to scrape up all the bat poop they could for Lexis's secret explosive recipe. She had already made a huge batch of it for this journey, and assured the 'Mites that carried it that they were totally safe, and it would only explode when she lit the long, twisted fuses they also carried. Builders and Diggers didn't question. They just carried on.

This distraction had to draw the Yellow Soldiers out of the Hive long enough for all the humans inside to escape. Then next month, when the moons rose together and triggered another pollen storm, we could use more of Lexis's explosives to collapse the Yellow Hive. Our Queen and our people would finally be safe.

Kinni was one of those left behind as we trooped out into the storm. She was obviously torn about Mo's decision not to bring her. Part of her was angry at being excluded, but part of her wanted nothing but to stay near the Queen.

We left them behind at the decaying Hive, and set off on our dangerous mission. A long parade of us snaked toward the Forbidden Zone. Mo and Lexis led the way, followed by a line of 'Mites, each touching the tail of the one in front with feelers, the only way they could follow. More humans interspersed down the line to make sure no one was left behind. I brought up the rear, marveling at the courage of our loyal 'Mites, trekking out, utterly blind, trusting us and our Queen's lingering scent.

As we walked, Lexis was full of questions, realizing that of all the humans who got the Queen's oil, only Kinni was affected. We had no answers, and Lexis wondered if it had anything to do with her being young and female. "There aren't any other female members of a Hive. One Queen at a time. Could our Queen have done something to the oil, to bind Kinni instead of anyone else? Maybe she thought she could be a threat if she became a Queen herself?" But there were other female humans that got the oil, including Lexis herself.

Each human carried empty woven bags. Holding them up in the air, we quickly filled them with flying pollen, tied them closed, and added them to the packs carried by the strong Diggers around us. By the time we reached the Forbidden Zone, every Digger was weighed down by bags of the dry, red dust.

It covered every surface. The plants that produced it grew over what I now knew were the remains of our transports and shuttles, destroyed not only by those early 'Mites who tore them apart in the first days after our people were taken captive, but also pummeled by the asteroid belt that surrounded our planet and occasionally dumped loads of burning rock from the gray sky.

Lexis took charge when we arrived.

"All right. We're going to try and lure them straight into the center." She pointed to a bare area in the middle of the huge ring of crushed ships. "That's where we'll need the trenches."

All our Diggers set to work. Directed by their human helpers, their huge claws scored out long divots in the hard ground. Brown dust from the excavation joined the pollen in the air.

I stood in the shadow of one of the huge transports. Its front half was caved in, enormous doors crushed and hanging open. Mo had said that in those early days, the 'Mites would keep Soldiers stationed inside the transports during the pollen storms to make sure our people couldn't return and collect any of the weapons they'd used in the initial ill-fated battle. All those guns and rockets had been hauled away from the site by the 'Mites, and the first time the escapees had tried to enter the transports to see what was left, they'd found an angry, venomous death waiting inside. They had never tried again.

This time we watched, though. From high on the hillside, our human lookouts made sure that no Soldiers were hiding in wait for us. The 'Mites must have assumed we'd long since forgotten about them. And looking at them now, I couldn't see what difference it would make. They were wrecked beyond hope of repair. All the doors hung open to the elements, and when I peered in, the shadows were a disaster. Dirt, pollen, and creeping vines covered everything. A thousand little animals must have made homes in the ships, insects and other creatures. Mo had described the kind of technology and equipment that the shuttles once held, and there was no way anything left behind would ever function again. Even if the holds were filled with rifles, the years of neglect would have made them useless.

Still, I wanted to see.

The isolation of my upbringing was a wall between me and all the other humans. I had learned so much about who and what humans really were. Travelers from a distant star. Masters of flight. Creators of magics I couldn't possibly have imagined. I thought back to the final test in the Ranking. The 'Mites had taken a chair from one of the derelict transport ships and brought it back to the Hive. They took it apart, and used it to see which of us were smart enough to figure out how to put it together again. The ones that were smart enough couldn't be allowed to survive. Queen's Service for anyone that might someday pose a threat. I had been smart enough, but compared to the things these humans knew, I was a fat gray seal playing in a river. They said I was human just like them, yet in my heart, I was still just a small, soft 'Mite. The human things Mo and Lexis talked about had no place in my mind. But this was my heritage.

I pushed aside the covering vines and hauled myself into the transport.

Dirt caked all the windows, and the shadowy shapes around me lost all meaning. I climbed over piles of unrecognizable garbage. *And would you recognize it even if it were whole and undisturbed? You didn't know what a chair was until you built one in the Hive.* All this stuff might look exactly like it was supposed to, and I'd never know.

There were rows of what were probably once seats, and along one wall hung a column of horizontal metal rungs. I looked up to where it led and saw a hatchway partly open to the sky. No wonder this one was such a mess. It had been raining inside for decades.

Boxes were smashed. Cloth stank of mildew and the small furry things that lived in this wreckage. My feet slipped on loose debris underfoot. I shuffled along, touching things that were totally alien to me. A piece of sharp metal cut my thumb and I sucked at the blood.

This could be useful. I made a mental note to see if our Diggers' claws could tear this sharp metal. We could make a lot more arrows if we had sharp metal points for them.

I stopped at the back wall. It was smooth and relatively undented. I peered out the dirty window along one side, watching our people work.

My hand lay flat on the wall, and I cocked my head. There was still a lot of transport left behind this wall. There had to be. By my reckoning, I had only walked about three quarters of the way down the length of the thing. Surely a lot more space lay behind this wall.

I felt along its surface until my fingers found a long, straight divot. It ran vertically, from the floor extending to higher than I could reach. Another similar divot was more than an arm's length away, and just to the right of that one was another irregularity.

I had no idea what it was.

Clearly all the 'Mites that were in here before me didn't either, because once I finally figured out to push my fingers under the hole and pull on the lever, the divots turned into a door that swung open.

CHAPTER 35

NOAH

I yelled for Lexis and Mo.

The room behind the door was packed full of stuff. In the dimness of the hold, I couldn't possibly determine what any of it was. Wouldn't have recognized it even if it were bright daylight, if I was honest.

Mo poked his head in. "What are you doing in there? It's not safe, Noah. This thing is a disaster."

"You need to see this," I said. "There's gotta be some stuff we can use here."

I didn't wait for Mo to clamber into the transport. This hold was full of things. The dust and small critters had taken a toll here as well, but there were large cubes of metal that looked intact. I ran my hands over the first one but couldn't figure out how to open it.

"What did you find?" Mo stood in the open doorway.

"Stars. They just left all this stuff?"

Dust swirled in the filtered light. "It was a door. I didn't know how to open it, but I figured it out. The 'Mites would have no idea what a door was. They would never figure out how to open one. It's just not how they are." Not how I was, either. But I was learning.

Lexis appeared behind Mo and together they crept into the hold.

"Some of these crates are still intact." They pried at the boxes, but nothing would budge.

"A Digger could open them," I suggested, but a Digger could never fit through the human-size door. How would these boxes have been unloaded? There must be some other entrance to this room, but before I could find it, Lexis said, "Oh, look! Tools!"

I didn't know what any of the things were that she pulled off the wall, but she seemed to know what to do with them. She and Mo set to prying open the crates.

"Seeds," she said. "Some of these might be useful if we ever get safe ground to plant them."

Mo pulled out a long, heavy roll of some flat, thin material. "Solar panel. Shame there's nothing to power anymore. No way anything that's sat this long in these conditions would ever work. And nobody knows how to fix it even if we found stuff."

A large crate in the back was painted with the same strange symbols that Kinni had shown me and sneered when I couldn't read them. As I thought about it, those same kinds of symbols were painted on the outsides of these transports. I'd seen them all my life and never known they were writing.

"Embryo storage," Mo said. "Well, that's a darned

shame."

I had no idea what that was, and when Lexis tried to explain that it was meant to bring babies from the old planet to this one, I started to think she was probably just making things up. I knew how big babies were. Only ten or twelve would fit inside the crate, and even over the dust and pollen, I would have been able to smell if there were babies in the box.

The next box made her whistle. "Oh, yeah. Screws. Nuts and bolts."

I looked to see giant boxes of the little metal tubes I had first seen when I put together the chair during the Ranking.

I didn't know why she was so happy, but even I could tell that the next few boxes were the jackpot.

The material was foreign to me, like everything else in this transport. But the first thing I pulled out was a long, thin tube, as tall as I was, with three sharp points made of heavy metal on the end.

I held it up like a spear. "Hey, look! There's a bunch of these!"

Mo and Lexis shuffled over.

"Pitchforks!" Mo shouted, and shoved me gently aside. He pulled out other similar tools. "Hoes and shovels. This is all farming equipment." He handed me a shovel. It was heavy, and although the edges weren't sharp, it would easily break the leg of an attacking Soldier. And the pitchforks . . .

"Imagine those spikes coated with Soldier venom," I said, eyeing the tools.

Lexis grinned in the thick air. "It's not what our ancestors intended. This stuff was all supposed to help us live in peace and work the land. We were supposed to be farmers, not warriors."

I grabbed a long, thin blade attached to a smooth handle. "Be careful with that," Mo said. "It's a machete."

Waving it around felt right in my hand, and I tucked it into the waistband of my pants. "I'm taking this with me."

Outside, the sounds of our Diggers trenching up the ground echoed between the crumpled metal hulls.

"None of this could possibly be what our ancestors intended," I said. "And once we get our people free, we'll have our chance to farm. We didn't start this war, but one way or another, we're going to end it."

CHAPTER 36

NOAH

By the time the pollen thinned in the air, we were on our way back to our Hive. Enough of the red dust still blew around to obscure our trail, which should buy us a few more days, but the Queen's scent was powerful. Even over the haze of pollen, the enemy Soldiers would find us soon.

We had buried most of the tools we found in another trench dug by our Diggers on the near side of the Forbidden Zone. Enough pollen mixed with the dirt they filled in that we hoped our scent wouldn't be more prevalent there than anywhere else. The Hive would know we'd been there, no doubt about that. But they couldn't possibly anticipate Lexis's plan.

The next three days were a frenzy of activity. Lexis supervised the distillation of more explosive powder. More 'Mites arrived, drawn from all around to commune with our

Queen. We didn't have time to give them all names, and it didn't matter.

Most of them wouldn't survive the battle.

The odds were against us. Everyone knew it. But we had to win. Without the people living in the bowels of the Hive, our numbers were too small. Even if those of us on the outside found somewhere safe to live, there weren't enough of us to carry on. In another generation, the only humans alive would be the Hive's slaves, living in ignorance. We didn't even know how many females and babies there were in the dark tunnels of the old Hive. But if we didn't rescue them, our survival wouldn't matter.

Kinni came into my room the night before I left on my part of the mission.

She flopped onto my bed next to me and I scooted down to give her room. I still had no idea what to make of her. Nothing in my upbringing prepared me to talk with a girl. She was part of our Hive now, and her scent soothed me, but she still made me trip over my tongue sometimes.

"So is it like this forever?"

I knew what she meant.

"For me it was a little different. I didn't get the oil right away. I shared her blood when she was sucked onto my belly." I rubbed the soft round scar on my belly, remembering the joy of having her as part of me.

She nodded. "I didn't understand. Thought you were completely mental. All I saw was a squishy maggot." Her eyes dropped in shame. "I couldn't imagine what could possibly make you risk your life for her."

"But you were all willing to. Even before you joined the Hive for real."

"It's different." She stretched out on my furs, kicking me in the shin. "We needed a Queen so we could try to make a safe place to life. It was just about survival." She nodded toward the open doorway. "Still is for them. But for me . . ."

I understood. "You would die for her. For any of us. Because we're a Hive."

She squirmed at the word. "Of course. And I can't explain it. Dad's been asking me questions since it happened. 'What does it feel like? Can you hear her in your head?'"

"There's no way to explain it to anyone that's not part of it."

From down the corridor, we heard the sounds of voices and the clicking of 'Mites as Lexis and Mo made their final plans.

"I thought it was some kind of weird mind-control thing," Lexis went on. "It seemed so creepy to me. Like she had part of your brain and was controlling you."

I smiled. It might look like that to an outsider.

"But it's not that," she said. "Not at all. I'm not controlled. She's not in my head. It's just that . . ." She searched for the words. "I love her, I guess. Not like I love my dad, and Lexis, and all the other people here. It's different. It's like she's part of my body."

A soft snort escaped my nose. "And you're part of hers. We all are. And each other, too."

She looked at me, and I looked away. She was part of my Hive. But she was still Kinni.

"You really think they'll come with you? The people in the big Hive?" she said.

I tugged at the bottom of my shirt. Human clothing still felt strange and scratchy. "They'll have to. Once I tell them the truth . . ." I trailed off. Would they believe me? What if they didn't?

"They think we're the enemy," she said, echoing my thoughts. "This whole thing hinges on getting them out of that Hive." Her fingers picked at the furs that made my sleeping pallet. "And not just the women and children." She looked straight at me. "A lot of us are going to die to give you this chance."

I wanted to protest that it wasn't my chance. It was all of our chances. Our only hope. But she was right. All of Lexis's planning was to draw the Soldiers out of the Hive and give me time to convince a bunch of clueless humans that everything they thought they knew about themselves was wrong, and they should follow me out of the only home they'd ever known. Leave the relative safety of the Masters' protection and hike out into a dangerous world. If we made it out and got them up into the mountain, they'd be safe. And the next pollen storm, Lexis and her explosives would bring the Hive down. We would build our own Hive near the ocean, and our Queen would produce our own Soldiers to defend us from any distant Hive that might someday try to attack us. But if the humans didn't believe my story, all the people and 'Mites providing the distraction would be fighting and dying for nothing. We would not escape this without heavy casualties. For our Queen and our future, we had no choice.

"Lexis has it under control," I said, hoping it was true. "Once I get the people out, she's got a bunch of the explosive ready to bring down the mountain pass behind us. By the time they get it dug out to come after us, it will be time for the next pollen storm. And that will be the end of them."

She sighed. "I hope you're right." A lock of her hair fell into her face and she shoved it behind her ear, changing the subject. "So they kept you apart, right? Older guys working and the young ones separate? Women and little kids on their own?"

I nodded.

"Did you know the younger boys? Were you all together?"

I shrugged. "We were kept in age groups, but I saw the younger boys. We all had jobs to do."

Her eyes filled with tears. "Did you know . . ." She stopped and sighed. "Their names were Grant and Joey, but of course the bugs wouldn't know that. And they were just babies. So who knows what their names would be if they lived."

A Soldier limped by the entrance to my chamber, missing a leg from the top joint. We had been extracting their venom for days, planning to coat the weapons we had and the pitchforks that waited for us in the Forbidden Zone. The Soldier paused, feelers waving, before lurching on down the tunnel.

Kinni continued. "I have two brothers. Had them, anyway. Twins. They were just babies when your Hive killed my mom. We think they took them, but . . ." Her eyes dropped. "They were twins. Maybe identical, but all babies look alike."

I thought for a moment.

"How long ago?"

"Nine years."

I thought about all the younger boys that had crowded around to hear my Ranking. That day seemed ages ago. Queen's Service. How proud I'd been to win the highest honor. *And how stupid.* Kinni's hair was long and yellow, unusual for our people. Most of us were varying shades of brown. I searched my memory of the afternoon I'd stood so tall in the sunlight.

"I think they're there," I said. "Two boys that look just alike, with hair like yours. I didn't know their names."

Her face lit up. "Grant and Joey. Doesn't matter what the bugs called them. They're my brothers." She gripped my arms, staring straight at me.

I couldn't look away.

"You have to bring them out, Noah. Promise me that no matter what else happens, if you can't get anybody else to come, promise that you'll bring my baby brothers out of that hell. I want them back. I want them to be part of our Hive."

Brothers. I knew what the word meant. And with a start, I realized the Hive was probably full of my brothers. All the boys were taken from the Mothers' Hall when we were very small. I now knew this was so that the original mothers couldn't pass on the knowledge of what had happened. They did this right from the beginning, and by the second generation, no one was left in the Hive that knew what they had done to us. Maybe the girls that stayed with their mothers had passed the story down, but they were never allowed out of their tunnels. And the boys that were chosen as Caretakers and went to live with them were never allowed out, either. Once the Masters pulled us from those chambers, we never returned. How many of the men that toiled for the Hive were my brothers or uncles? Did I have more brothers even now, working as hard as they could to please the insects that had stolen their heritage?

Chen.

They'd taken him to be a Caretaker, to live with the women and babies.

Maybe Chen knew the truth.

I couldn't imagine the anguish. When they dragged him down away from the sunlight for the last time, he would have had no idea. Did the women in that dungeon know? Had they kept the knowledge of what humans once were alive down there, powerless to escape? Would it be worse if they knew, or if they shared the ignorance of the boys that served the Hive, working ourselves to early death for the Masters that had made our whole lives a pathetic lie?

I looked at Kinni. She had lived her whole life free, running from camp to camp, watching for the one mistake that would doom them all. She had never known safety. But she had always known freedom.

And me? I had been safe, to a point. Living in a Hive, even a sick, putrid one like the one I'd grown up in, was safer than anywhere else in the world. We did what we were told, and we paid for that safety with our lives, but if we could only succeed . . . I pictured it. A brand new Hive, led by our perfect Blue Queen. 'Mites and humans living together, working for the good of the whole. Each of us would toil for all of the others, and we would have plenty to share. Our Soldiers would keep us secure from invaders. Our Diggers would burrow deep into the ground, and our Builders would make great, circling towers into the sky. All around, humans would dive, and clean, and . . . No. Not just the roles given to us by the Masters. No more Runners, pushing themselves to early deaths under an unforgiving sun. No more Divers like Miguel, so eager to please his overlords that he would swim beyond his strength and drown, unmourned by the creatures whose approval he died for. We would create things, like Lexis and her explosives. We would write things with juice on bark so that our stories would never be forgotten. And we would make the Hive better. Stronger. Smarter. We could all do it together.

I smiled at Kinni, full of the wonder of my dreams.

"I promise. No matter what, I'll get your brothers out."

CHAPTER 37

NOAH

We all trooped out together.

I led our ragtag army of humans and 'Mites, walking next to Mo on one side and our Queen on the other. She was growing fast, and was almost as tall as me now when she stood up on her hind legs. In the early morning, we all received her blessing, anointing ourselves with the pure blue-scented oil from her head. She had learned a lot of words, clicking along with me and the others who knew the shared language. But we didn't need words. We were bonded together from the sharing of my blood. I was hers and she was mine, and with every step we took toward the hateful ground of our enemy, the anger inside me simmered hotter, blue-purple waves flowing behind me.

They wanted to kill her. And for this reason, I wanted to kill them.

I wore only the pants I had been given, with the machete belted around my waist. Bare feet slapping against the ground, I plowed toward my destiny.

On the top of the mountain pass, we parted ways.

My mission was a solo run. The path to the underground river where I would swim into the hated Hive lay farther away to the south. Once I dropped into the water, I would make much better time than the crowd of fighters who were heading to the plateau on our side of the Forbidden Zone. By the time I emerged in the subterranean pool, the enemy Soldiers would be streaming out of the Hive, drawn by the smell of our Queen. The Builders and Diggers left behind wouldn't fight me. Neither would the humans. Some of the men might be pulled into the battle, but we couldn't help that. There would be casualties today. Lexis had seen to that.

We stopped in the pass.

I looked back at the line of people and 'Mites. This was our future. We had already proven it could be done—humans and insects living together, working together. Our Blue Queen didn't care which species we were. Every member of our Hive was hers, even if the other humans besides me and Gil and Kinni didn't feel the bond like we did. If we succeeded today, we could make it work. But so much could go wrong.

Mo startled me with a hug. "We're all counting on you, Noah," he said. "Please, please bring back my sons."

Kinni must have told him.

Lexis gave me an awkward one-armed hug. "You can do it. We'll keep them busy."

I nodded. There wasn't room for the rest of the people and 'Mites to cluster around me in the narrow pass, and I was just as glad. Too many hugs would throw off our timing. I didn't want a hug from Gil, though my feelings about him were much kinder since the Queen had made him her own.

The Queen approached me.

"Goodbye," I clicked. In reality, the human/insect language was far too simple for a concept like, "Goodbye." What I really said was, "Eat well." But she knew what I meant.

She touched me with her soft feelers, and exuded her warm scent. Her head lowered and I took one last touch of the precious oil, rubbing it on my chest where my heart fluttered at her affection.

I would do this for her. For Chen. For Kinni and for Sunshine. I would do this for all of humankind, and all the 'Mites who would come after us.

The sky was clear blue as I left the group and jogged toward destiny.

The recent pollen storm had washed away all the scent trail leading back to the river's entrance. I was guided by the deeper smell of fresh water and wet rock. No trace remained where Sunshine had waited for me the last time I made this swim, but I recognized the little cove. The rocks were slippery as I clambered down to the flowing river. Tiny lizards and thousand-legged worms scuttled out of my way. One large rock jutted out over the current. This was where Sunshine had pulled me from the water, nearly dead. Today I was alone, but a member of a Hive was never truly alone. I felt them in my heart. They were counting on me.

Cold splash into the water. Today it would be a one-way swim. By the time I arrived in the Hive, the Soldiers should be gone. I would rush to the Mothers' Chambers and find all the women and children. They, along with any other boys and men we could convince to join us, would follow me out of the Hive and around the Forbidden Zone to the south. We would travel up a different pass higher in the mountains and await the other humans in a safe cave, too high for 'Mites to follow. Our 'Mites would return to our fortified Hive, and once the women and children were safe, I would join them and the other fighters. Lexis had a plan to detonate her explosives and cover their retreat, but if the enemy found their trail, we would hold them off until the next pollen storm drove them back home. Then we would bury them forever with one final blast. Our Queen and our people would be safe.

With one deep breath, I dropped beneath the surface. The current pulled me along, and my mind quieted in the easy flow. *Left. Right. Center and down.* I paused in sunlit pools to suck in air, and grabbed at the rock ceiling for gulps of breath in tiny columns of light, pressing my face into little crevasses and clinging to the stone. *Left. Left.*

As I floated, I thought about what I might say to convince the captives who didn't even know they were captive. How could I possibly distill what I'd learned into something that would fit in the short time I'd have to make them understand? What if they were too afraid to follow me? What if they thought I was lying, as they'd been lied to their whole lives? What if they didn't want freedom?

All too soon I was there.

The moment I broke the surface of the river inside the

Hive, I was overwhelmed by the stench. Yellow and filthy, the air choked me. How had I lived here my entire life and never realized how rotted this place was? The old, sick Queen's stench was everywhere. My mouth filled with a wash of saliva and bile filled my throat. I gulped with a grimace, climbing out of the pool. The smear of my Blue Queen's oil had almost completely washed away in the river, and my heart ached for her healthy, vibrant scent.

Steady. Don't be overwhelmed. Make sure it's time.

I closed my eyes and breathed in, sniffing and listening. The smell of alarm was everywhere here, and the vibration of hundreds of Soldiers on the move told me that our challenge was being answered.

Wait. Give them time to get out.

I counted backwards from a hundred, one number for each breath. By the time I reached one, the scuttling above me had quieted, and the stench of Soldiers had begun to clear. The Hive was nearly empty of the 'Mites I once called Masters.

It was time to rescue my people.

CHAPTER 38

NOAH

Up and up, through tunnels I once knew only by sight. I breathed through my mouth, but it didn't help. The yellow, rancid smell of death crept into the back of my burning throat.

Get the people. And get out.

A few 'Mites skittered around the corners, but by scent alone I knew they were Diggers. They all tried to crowd me, feelers waving at my chest.

I must still carry a bit of her scent.

None of them tried to stop me, and I pushed through them, clicking "Come. New Queen." I didn't know if they would join us, but any who didn't would be killed when the Hive collapsed next pollen time.

We wove up through the Hive, an ever-lengthening parade with me at the head. Together we became one of the thousand-legged bugs, flowing toward the Mothers' Chambers.

At the entrance to those forbidden tunnels, I paused. I had never been down there before. The way was unfamiliar. In the distance, the dim light of glowstones shone from rooms along the hallway, but I didn't need eyes to show me the way. The scent of closely packed humans was a beacon.

The two Diggers at the entrance touched me with their feelers and let me pass. They were never here to keep anyone out. Only in.

I could smell a large, open chamber straight ahead. As I passed smaller rooms on each side, people peered from the shadows. Women and babies.

"Come on," I said to each little group. "We all need to be together now."

They followed, carrying small crying bundles on their hips. Toddlers clustered around my legs and the parade of 'Mites swelled with people.

At the end of the tunnel, a huge room stank of too many people too close together. It was brighter than the smaller chambers, with isolated shafts of light streaming in through air passages that led to the surface.

"Noah?"

I peered into the gloom. His scent was unfamiliar to me, but I knew his voice.

"Chen!" I forgot my carriage as ambassador for my Hive. Chen was here, alive.

He raced across the room and skidded to a halt in front of me.

I grinned and threw my arms around him. "I've come to save you!"

A look of wonder covered his features and his hand reached up to touch his chest where I had embraced him. He breathed in the faint scent of my Queen. All around me, the women and children sighed, crowding as close as they could to me.

I'd prepared a long speech. I had planned to tell them all about our ships from the stars, about the treachery of the Masters, about the chance for freedom with our people. A good sniff told me all that was unnecessary. The scent of blue hung faintly around the bowls left over from their breakfast.

My Queen had developed in a vat of algae. She lived there for days before I came to rescue her, imbuing it with the oils from her body. Every human in this Hive ate that algae.

They were already hers.

All I said was, "The Queen is outside. Come with me and join her."

They followed with dreamy joy on their faces.

We emerged from the tunnel that led to the Mothers' Chambers. On the way up toward the surface, groups of younger boys joined our many-legged walk. "Come to the new Hive," I told them, and they trotted along with us.

In the large chamber near the entrance, we paused, gathering into a group. I looked around and realized there were a hundred people crowded in, surrounded by Diggers and Builders. The women were blinking, pale and squinting into the bright light. They clutched each other and their babies, fear warring with hope in their eyes.

"We're going out, and we're not coming back. There's a new Queen. Young and healthy. There's a new way to live. Fresh air and sunlight. We live with the Masters as equals, not as slaves."

Their blank stares told me what I must have looked like when I was rescued and told the truth.

Chen was next to me. "They told me everything," he said, nodding at the women. "We're angels that fell from the stars, cast into the darkness for our wickedness. Only through service can we someday hope to return to the sky."

What is he talking about?

"Um, not exactly," I said. "We're actually aliens from another planet, enslaved by a species that stole our history and made us believe we were inferior to them." The original mothers would have known that. But over the years, the story must have changed. Now they looked at me as if I'd flown in on dragonfly wings to carry them straight into the sky. Kinni would have said: *whatever works.* I smiled at the people. "The new Queen is waiting for us." That was good enough.

Noise from deep in the tunnel pricked my ears. I sniffed the dank air.

Soldiers. Time to go.

Not many. But it wouldn't take many. These people weren't fighters. Unarmed, they were shellfish waiting to be plucked from the sea. I peered among them, looking for two identical faces.

Kinni's brothers weren't there.

Chen wouldn't know what happened. He'd been locked away in the Mothers' Chambers. I searched the room for a boy who looked about the right age. "You there. I'm looking for two boys that look exactly the same. I don't know their names, but I know they were here when I left. Where are they?"

The boy stared at me. "Matthew and Martin?"

"Sure. I guess so. About your age?"

He nodded. "They're gone."

My heart sank. I'd promised.

The boy continued. "They were messing around with stuff, started drawing with berry juice on the walls of our room. Making pictures."

We weren't allowed to do anything like that. When I'd lived here, I'd thought it was because the Masters wanted everything to look the same. Now I realized they didn't want us developing a written language.

"When?" I demanded. "When did they take them away?" *Please, please, please.* I knew where they would have been sent.

"Yesterday."

Hope flared in my heart. Yesterday. They would still be alive down there.

I turned to Chen.

"You have to lead them. Get them out of here." I told him where to go, skirting the Forbidden Zone where the fighting would be happening right now. How long would our people keep the Hive's Soldiers busy? How many had they killed? How many of ours had already died?

The Diggers and Builders wouldn't fight for us here. They would follow me out, or stay here, but without the bond to a Queen they had never met, they would never defend us. I clicked for two of them to follow me.

I sniffed again. At least three Soldiers. Maybe four.

Coming straight up the tunnel behind me.

"Go now," I said, giving Chen a shove. "Get them out. Run for the mountains and I'll catch up with you. Go!"

He opened his mouth to protest, then looked up at the bright sunlight streaming in through the doorway. "Eat well." He dashed out the door, and the people followed him at my urging.

I turned into the dark tunnel and drew my machete.

CHAPTER 39

KINNI

It started out so well.

By the time we got to the landing site where the ships of our ancestors sat ruined and crumbling, the slaver bugs knew we were coming. We could see them in the distance, boiling out of their huge Hive, and skittering through the grassland toward the empty ground between the ships.

We barely had enough time to unload the explosives.

Our Diggers and Builders were laden with individual bags of the powder Lexis had made. Each one had a long, woven string attached to it, which we would light on fire before throwing the bag at the trenches our bugs had dug and lightly covered with dirt.

They trusted us so much.

Or maybe they just trusted the little Queen. She barely talked in the clicking language we shared, but she didn't have to. I hadn't understood until the oil. I thought Noah was crazy, addled from living his whole life as a slave. The thought made my eyes roll back. He lived in a Hive, but was denied the oil. To be so close, to know there was a bond he didn't share . . . No wonder he was crazy.

And I was crazy now, too. Noah was over the top in love with the Queen. I felt it, too. Devotion to her, and from her. She adored us all just as we adored her. Separately we were nothing, but bonded together we had the strength of a mountain. There was no psychic bond. I couldn't feel pain when another 'Mite was hurt or anything. *Another 'Mite.* Like I was just another bug. But in some ways I felt more akin to the other 'Mites than to my people now. Marching beside my blue-scented Queen, next to my Hivemates, I felt invincible. And if Noah succeeded in his mission, my brothers might get the chance to feel the connection I had never realized I needed in my life.

They were in there. He'd seen them.

Sorrow for their lost childhood and rage at what the Yellow Queen took away simmered in my veins at the thought. I'd long since given up hope. But Noah knew them. They were alive. And if today went well, they'd be free tonight.

"Wait," Lexis cautioned.

We were all poised and ready, cloth bag-bombs in hand. She had lit a couple of torches and stuck them in the dirt so we could light the fuses and hurl them off when the time was right. Too early, and we'd lose our chance.

"Wait," she said, squinting across the field.

The first bugs were swarming into the clearing. My heart dropped as I looked behind them. From the front line all the way back to where the Hive rose in the distance, the ground was alive with them, sickly yellow. The whole valley stank with their rotten Queen's odor.

"So many," I murmured. "Way more than we thought."

Lexis's face was grim. My dad stood next to her, mirroring her tight lips.

They're scared.

They should be.

We're all gonna die.

Or worse, I thought, squeezing the bag of explosive powder in my hands. *I'm a girl. They probably won't kill me. They'll probably drag me back into their Hive and lock me away forever. Away from my Queen. I'll churn out baby slaves in that putrid hole for the rest of my life, and they'll grow up thinking that's the way it's supposed to be. They'll never know a real Hive.*

No. I gritted my teeth and looked out at the oncoming swarm. *I'd much rather die on this hillside today.*

Our people were armed, with skins full of bug venom tied at their waists. Pitchforks and sharpened shovels with the paralytic neurotoxin against a thousand huge insects with stingers full of the stuff. Bows sat with piles of arrows.

This was totally insane.

"Ready . . ." Lexis said, and we all tensed.

The first bugs were almost all the way to the edge of the trenches we'd made. We had to time this perfectly, or it was over before it began.

"On three we light. On one we throw."

I raised my bomb toward the torch. Everyone else crowded around and did the same.

"Five, four . . ." Lexis counted. "Three."

We stuck our fuses into the fire.

"Two, and . . . one."

Every one of us threw our bombs down onto the leading edge of the trenches.

The blast knocked me back onto my butt. I scrambled to all fours and looked out over the field.

Over half of the trenches we'd dug had blown. We'd filled them with Lexis's gunpowder, all the nails, screws, bits of broken metal, and shrapnel we could find, along with giant bags of dried pollen from the last storm.

There were bug parts everywhere.

A cheer went up from our side as we beheld the carnage. The blast had blown some bugs clean apart, while the shrapnel cut others to ribbons. A thick, red, smoky haze hung over the field where the bugs in the back that weren't harmed were suddenly blinded in the field. The stench of the Yellow Soldiers blown to bits, and the hot, smoky smell of the gunpowder brought bile to the back of my throat.

"Charge!"

I barely heard my dad's voice. We barreled down the hill, weapons raised, screaming like maniacs. I tore into the center of the bugs, chopping with my shovel, knocking them back and severing limbs. I had no idea if the venom on the edge was doing anything at all as I swung the heavy tool, a one-woman thresher in a field of rotten wheat.

Yellow bugs were everywhere, slamming into each other and us. Red sweat ran down my arms. I was pollen-coated death. Fifteen years of rage poured out with every stroke of my shovel. *For my mother. For my brothers. For every person that landed on these ships thinking they'd found a home. For the idiot back in that Hive who better be getting our people out of there.* I couldn't feel my arms or legs. Only the clang of the shovel hitting another of my enemies. *For my Hive. For my Queen.*

"Kinni, help me!"

Lexis's voice cut through my battle haze. She was calling from above me, clinging to the side of one of the crushed ships.

I whacked a bug that staggered in my direction and dashed over to where Lexis hung.

"Get up here, I need you!" she called.

I didn't want to leave my shovel, but it was too big to carry. Lexis wouldn't ask if it wasn't life or death. The shovel landed on the ground with a puff of pollen and I scrambled up the side of the transport to Lexis.

"Come with me and bring these! We have to get more of the trench to explode!"

We'd dug the trenches in hope that one blast at the front edge would cause a chain reaction and blow them all the way across the field. But the explosions had stopped in the middle, and more bugs were pouring in from the grassland.

The ship was a wreck, and I clutched as many of the bombs as I could carry, stumbling across the top. Cratered and halfway caved-in, the transport was a twisted, overgrown obstacle course. But I grew up on the run. I overtook Lexis and rushed to the back of the transport.

From above, the situation was grim. All our 'Mites were spread around our side of the field, staying out of the hazy pollen cloud. When one of the enemies would stagger out blind, ours would rush in and attack.

But we were losing. There were just too many.

"Here!" Lexis snapped me back to the transport. "Light them up!"

She held the torch and I lit the fuses, hurling bomb after bomb over the side toward the shallow trenches. With every explosion we ducked down under the raised edge, shielding our faces from the flying nails and screws. The smell of death was overpowering and filled me with glee.

I peered over at the carnage, my sense of smell numbed by the smoke billowing around. *Is she all right?* I squinted into the distance. Standing on top of the hillside, twenty of our bugs stood guard over our Queen.

And still the enemies came. Whether they were still being drawn by the smell of our young Queen, or whether the sounds and smells of the battle had blotted her out, they flooded into the kill zone.

I threw the last of our bombs.

In the far distance, a shadow moved over the hills. They were much too distant for me to pick out any individuals, but with a flare of hope, I realized what I was seeing.

"Look! They're free!"

Lexis followed my pointing finger. A line of humans straggled out to the south of the battle, heading toward the lower mountain pass.

He'd done it. He got them out. My brothers, and all the rest. Just a bit longer and they'd be safe. We could all make our escape back into the hills and wait for the next pollen storm to end this once and for all.

And then the wind picked up.

I watched with horror as the haze of pollen blew away from the killing field. There were still so many bugs. Some were injured, but so were some of ours. Our people were suddenly exposed as the bugs' sense of smell returned, along with my own.

"Retreat! Retreat!" Lexis's voice was joined by mine, and every other human that heard the call.

We raced back across the transport. A line of explosive had been planted all around the entrance to the pass we would use to escape once our people were safe. As soon as we were all through, we'd use one last bomb to blow it, causing a rockfall from above and destroying our trail.

I looked up to the plateau that led to the pass.

Enemy bugs were swarming up the hillside.

Our Queen was surrounded.

Our escape path was cut off.

I was right.

We were all going to die.

CHAPTER 40

CHEN

I led our people out into the light. At the entrance to the Hive, I paused a moment, breathing in the fresh air. Everything smelled so vibrant. I remembered the scent of the ocean from what seemed like ages ago when I last stood under the open sky. But there were so many layers to it. Dry sand, baking in the sun. Clear water on top, and deeper turmoil below. Something dead far out of sight, some sea creature washed up on the shore.

"Chen?" My sister Glenna took my arm, her baby in the other. "He said to go to the mountains. The messenger."

I grinned. "He's not a messenger from the sky. He's Noah. My best friend." I glanced back at the Hive. The scent Noah had carried on his skin had awakened me like never before. The Hive behind was dying, wretched. Our time here was finished. "But he's come to save us, that's for sure."

We turned and filed around the Hive, leaving the ocean behind us. Noah had told me to go through the field toward the Forbidden Zone, then skirt around it toward a pass in the mountains. Someone would be there to meet us and lead us higher into the hills where we would be safe. I wasn't certain if this was the moment all the mothers had been waiting for, but I knew I was never setting foot in that Hive again. Wherever Noah was sending us, we were going.

The smell of battle reached me long before the sound. The glorious blue scent Noah had carried, that I'd been tasting without knowing it for weeks, drifted across the grassland. With it came the sick, yellow stench of the Soldiers I'd once thought of as my own. There was blood and death, venom and pollen, and a strange, hot smell I had never encountered before.

I led our people across the plain and up onto the edge of the big canyon of the Forbidden Zone. The mothers went crazy when we reached the edge, pointing at the huge, hulking shapes that now swarmed with Masters and feral humans.

"There!" Shari cried. She was supported by two of the men, heavy with her impending delivery. "It's the place! We have to go down there to get our wings!"

I looked down the hill. Battle raged, and the confusing sounds and sights warred in my brain. "No way. Noah said to go around." I pointed to the mountains in the distance. "He said to go there."

"But this is the place from the story," she said, panting with excitement and the long walk. "That's where we have to go."

An explosion of light and heat filled the air between the

giant shapes with pollen and flying bits of metal. The death smell filled the air, and the feral humans charged into the chaos.

"If anyone goes down there right now, they're not coming back up," I said.

I turned to the people behind me. I loved their story, but like the rest of the men who had spent their childhoods away from it, the words didn't carry the same power over me as they did for the women who were steeped in it from birth and never left to forget it. Maybe we were angels. Maybe somehow we would learn to fly. But not down there, and not today.

"Look," I said, and pointed up to the mountains again. "That's where the messenger said to go. He told us to go up that mountain pass, and another messenger would lead us higher. That's got to be the right thing. From way up there, we'll be able to look straight down over the Forbidden Zone, and when we get our wings, we'll be able to fly right over it. I'm sure that's what the story meant."

After long moments of murmuring, the people began to nod.

"I think we need to go down there," Shari said. "But not yet. I think there's more we must do to prove our worth. The messenger said to go up. So we'll go up."

I relieved one of the men helping her, slinging an arm under her shoulder. We trooped away from the edge where the battle raged below.

So many Ferals. I'd had no idea. And Noah had said the new Queen was out here. I smelled her, far across the war zone, and longed to run to her. But even if I made it, the women and children behind me never would.

One day, I'll come to you. And even if I never fly, I'll be content to see you just once.

Our progress was slow, but the people were strong. We took turns supporting the women who were heavy with babies, and carried the toddlers on our hips. Most of the younger boys had joined us, the unranked, along with most of the Ranked men of the Hive. There were plenty of strong backs to share the load. The men and boys didn't know the women's truth, and had no idea where we were going, or why. But one sniff of the glorious smell on Noah, and they would follow his directions.

The fighting in the Forbidden Zone fell away below us as we climbed. Just around a bend, out of sight of the valley, a Feral woman stepped out of the shadows.

"You made it out!" she said, and looked over our number. "Oh, my. You're exhausted, poor thing. Let's get you somewhere safe." She was talking to my pregnant sister Shari, who looked about to drop.

Two Diggers skittered out from behind the Feral woman. They all shared Noah's Queen's smell. The Masters were each missing their giant claws, but their hind legs were intact. They weren't from our Hive. The Feral woman helped us push Shari and one of the other women onto the backs of the Masters where they clung, shivering.

"The 'Mites can't take us all the way up," the woman said. "Too cold for them. But we'll get you as high as we can. Rest and hang on, and let's get you somewhere safe."

I waited until the last of my people had filed up the narrow path, and followed the last child up into the clouds.

CHAPTER 41

NOAH

While Chen led the people outside to freedom or death, I turned and raced down the tunnels. The two Diggers I'd commandeered followed along, drawn by the sweet scent of our healthy Queen coming from my skin.

The farther down I ran, the more my blood boiled.

This Hive's old, sick Queen was enraged. Her smell was the color of fire now, orange and red. She could smell me. She knew I was here. The scents she was secreting filled the deep corridors with bitter wrath. I squinted my eyes shut, inhaling her fury in the darkness. The tunnels of this place were well-worn by years of 'Mite feet, leaving their scent trails everywhere. I didn't need to see. I knew exactly where I was going, down the empty, back tunnels that led straight to the larva pools.

A single Soldier burst out of a tunnel just ahead of me.

No doubt it could smell me, smell my Queen on me. But the advantage was all mine. It expected a slave. What it got was a madman.

The machete caught a glint of the dim glowstones as I raised it and charged. The Soldier didn't have time to whip its tail around before I launched myself straight at its head. The power of my jump and the sharpness of my blade combined into one savage stroke. The Soldier's head dropped neatly from its thorax. Its mandibles clicked and its body thrashed for a moment before falling still.

I took a moment to chop straight into its tail. A sharp, acid scent filled the air as I coated my blade with the dead Soldier's paralyzing venom.

The two Diggers behind me scuttled over the body, clicking in alarm.

I could smell that my hold on them was waning. Far below, the hated Queen was spewing her own acid stench, red rage filling the tunnels. The Diggers were getting fearful.

They should be afraid. Of me.

"Follow!" I clicked, and bolted down the corridor.

I took a zigzagging path, hoping to throw the Soldiers still in the Hive off my trail. Nearly all the Soldiers had obviously been drawn out to the Forbidden Zone where I hoped Mo and Lexis were holding them off long enough for Chen to get the rest of our people clear. This detour was never part of our plan, though. If they detonated their escape screen and fled over the hills while I was still down here, all the Soldiers would flood back into the Hive. I could slip away through the rivers, but Kinni's brothers would never be able to follow me. They'd be paralyzed, and even if I could get them down to the open water, I would never be strong enough to tow them upstream to a safe pool.

Hurry. No time.

The Diggers followed me down and down. At the bottom of the tunnel, the familiar splash of the shallow pools echoed around the walls. The nearest pools had been cleaned out since I was dragged through, my belly laden with eggs. The dead husks of seals and humans were gone, and the first pool was empty. In the second one, I found the boys.

"Matthew? Martin?" I whispered. They couldn't nod, but their panicked eyes told me everything. The eggs on their bellies hadn't hatched yet, but the next few pools held seals that weren't as lucky.

Sticky white goo glued the eggs to their skin. I dragged them up out of the water and scraped the eggs onto the floor. The smell down here was overpowering. We were so close to the Queen. She knew it and was white hot fury, trapped in the room she'd grown to fill. I could hear her thrashing in the next chamber, and smell the red summons she emitted. Her Soldiers would be here soon.

"Pick up," I clicked to the Diggers. "Bring."

Matthew and Martin were dead weight. I couldn't possibly carry them, but the Diggers could. They scooped the boys up and I stepped back, crushing one of the sticky eggs on the ground with a wet pop.

It smelled like her inside. Sick. Yellow. Full of anger and pride.

Red haze clouded my eyes. I stomped through the room, popping eggs, grinding the half-developed larvae inside under my bare feet. Sticky goo squished between my toes and its touch drove me insane with the need to kill. The scent enraged my Hive sense. And the memory of being left down here to die, sucked dry for another generation of sick Yellow 'Mites, made me rage for the generations of slavery that took my identity away.

Human. I was human. Not a Lowform. Not a Feral. A human, and even more than that, the first human member of a Hive. The blood of both species roared in my veins.

When all the eggs from the boys were squashed, I raced to the next pool and ripped the larvae off the seals that lay there paralyzed. Stomp and squish. They tried to wriggle away but I was a tornado of hatred. My legs were caked up to the knees in the guts of my enemies, and still I was not sated. The smell of the nearby Queen's rage mixed with my own, and my ears rang with a screaming din, blood pounding in my veins.

When I finally looked up from my furious destruction, both of the Diggers had backed into a corner, holding the limp boys close to their bodies.

And three Soldiers, along with the Hive's King, burst into the room.

CHAPTER 42

NOAH

They dashed straight at me.

I raised my machete and charged.

All three of the Soldiers pounded forward together while the small, unarmed King hung back. Behind me, the Diggers holding the boys cowered into the corners.

I splashed through a shallow pool right at the Soldiers. At the last moment I tucked and rolled to my right, slashing out with my machete. It sliced through a leg of the rightmost Soldier, and sent it toppling to the ground.

My shoulder was on fire where I had landed, but I scrambled to my feet. The downed Soldier was struggling in the pool as the venom from my blade made one side of it go limp. There wasn't enough to completely immobilize it, but it scuttled in a circle, clicking with rage.

The other two split up, one coming in from each side.

I dashed to the left and scooped up the severed leg of the Soldier, flinging it right at the face of the one coming straight at me. It dodged the projectile and I jumped past it. I hoped to repeat the single-stroke victory I'd scored in the tunnel, but my blade bounced off the hard thorax and I spun around from the force. Its swinging tail just missed me as I tumbled to the ground and rolled away.

The other Soldier was right behind me, waving its sharp pincers my way. I jumped up and ran back toward the Diggers, machete arm tingling from the blow.

Two thick, furry bodies darted past me. The two seals, freed from their parasites, were drunkenly flopping away as the toxin wore off, heading for the sound of open water. The Soldier stumbled over them and crashed just behind me.

"Look out!"

I heard the voice and spun around as the Soldier slid over to me.

My machete found its home. The enemy's head spun free from its body.

One down.

I realized that the Soldiers weren't great fighters. There was nothing on the planet that threatened them besides other Hives, and this Hive hadn't seen battle for decades. It ruled the land for miles. This was certainly the first time these Soldiers had ever been in a real fight.

It wasn't mine.

The boys were regaining some movement, squirming in the Diggers' grasp. One had obviously regained his voice and shouted to me a second ago.

"Stay there!" I yelled to them. "We're getting you out!"

The partially paralyzed Soldier was limping toward me,

and the one I'd hit in the chest dashed around to my side. I lurched away from its swinging tail and stumbled into the Digger holding Matthew. It dropped the boy and staggered to the side, spinning around between me and the attacking Soldier.

I don't think it meant to save my life. It was probably just trying to get away. But when the Soldier's tail swung with a lethal dose of venom, it hit the Digger square in the belly. It crumpled to the ground.

I launched myself over its back and swung at the Soldier. Its stinger was stuck in the Digger's body and I chopped down, severing the tail. Acid venom splashed all around and hit me in the left eye.

My vision on that side dimmed and my lips felt fat and heavy.

Hurry. End it before you go down. Save the boys.

"Get out of here!" I called to the boys, but my face wouldn't work, and what came out was garbled.

The Soldier threw its body at me. Without a stinger it couldn't paralyze me with venom, but it was three times my weight and plated with armor. It could still kill me with a single blow.

I raised the machete before me.

The Soldier landed on me, machete impaling its chest. It thrashed, grinding my back into the hard stone floor, and was still. Its weight crushed me and I couldn't breathe. *This is it. I hope they get away.*

With an agonizing shift, the dead Soldier's weight was dragged off me. I looked up to see the remaining Digger, heavy claws grasping the dead Soldier.

It saved me!

With an enraged click, it drove a claw right at my head. I rolled away as it crashed into the floor.

Not a rescue. My Queen's scent was overpowered by theirs. This Digger was no longer mine to command.

I grabbed for the machete and scuttled away.

The venom in my eye was already wearing off, and I blinked to clear my head.

The Soldier that was half-crippled by venom limped toward me. It was slow, but so was I. My blade connected with the legs on its good side, and it went down, tail swinging wildly, splashing up water from the warm pool.

Behind me the Digger raised its claws.

"Look out!"

A rain of glowstones knocked the Digger away. Both boys had dragged themselves around the edge of the room and were pelting the creature with anything they could grab.

Above me, the tunnels filled with scuttling sounds.

All the Diggers and Builders were crashing down the corridors. And I didn't smell like a healthy Queen anymore.

From the chamber beyond, the enemy Queen's red rage scent filled the room. She called to her 'Mites with smell, and they were coming.

She was the cause of all of this.

She had lived too long. When our ships arrived from the stars, she had given the order to attack, to take our people as slaves to the Hive. Because of our labor, she'd grown huge and lived for decades, creating an empire that never should have taken over this land.

She took my childhood. She was killing my friends even now.

She had tried to kill me.

It was time for her to die.

"Get out of here. Run away to the mountains," I said to the boys. "My people will find you."

Leaving the angry Digger and the legless, flopping Soldier in the pool, I rushed toward the Queen's chamber.

The small, unarmed King jumped in front of me and I kicked him away. There wasn't a true door into the Queen's chamber from here, but a small crack in the wall, which I slipped through.

She filled the chamber with fury. Eight legs thrashed toward me, her huge, fat tail whipping around. But it held no venom, and she couldn't kill me with eggs.

I launched myself at her, climbing up her body. She beat me with her tail, but I hung onto my machete. Her body lurched to the side, crushing mine into the wall. A shower of dirt and grime pelted us from above and I slipped back down to her tail.

Outside the chamber, the Digger was frantically clawing at the crack I'd slipped through, trying to dig its way through to us. Great chunks of the wall crumbled to dust.

Do it. Do it now.

The Digger would be through in seconds. When it got to me, it would kill me.

I wouldn't go alone.

Once again, I vaulted up the Queen's back, climbing her useless, waving legs. She flung herself from side to side, but I hung on, my fury matching hers. When I reached her shoulders, I clicked to her in a language I didn't even know if she understood.

"Dead. Now."

One perfect swing.

The hated Slaver Queen's head toppled from her body onto the sticky ground below.

CHAPTER 43

KINNI

Enemy Soldiers surrounded our Queen. She was up there on the plateau that was supposed to be our escape route, along with a handful of our Soldiers and a couple of the men. The enemies were pouring up the edges of the hill on each side, squeezing our fighters toward the steep edge leading out to the open plain. All I could do was watch in horror as all our plans dissolved second by second.

We would never get another chance. Never get another Queen.

A sob choked my throat at the thought of losing her when I'd just found her.

I knew some humans would make it through the day. Noah had gotten the people out of the Hive. If any of Lexis's explosive powder—or Lexis herself—managed to survive this, they could still blow up the Hive next pollen time, assuming the Yellow bugs didn't hunt them down before that. None of the new Hive people would know how to make it. They didn't even know how to read.

"Lexis, you have to get out of here!" I screamed over the noise.

She was staring at the plateau where our people were backing right up to the edge.

"Lexis!" I repeated, but she wasn't listening.

"They're coming over," she said, and I followed her gaze.

She was right. More than half of the enemy Soldiers had streamed up the sides of the high plateau. Now the first of ours leaped over the edge, sliding down the steep front face and crashing into the hard ground below. The stench of terror washed across the field.

It was hardest on the humans. They didn't have eight legs to grab at the earth during the skid, and we didn't have an exoskeleton to bounce at the bottom like a 'Mite did. The humans at the bottom of the steep slope didn't move. But the 'Mites did.

The Queen jumped. My heart sank with her as she fell, tumbling down and down. The Soldiers we had left, human and 'Mite, met her at the bottom and started fighting off the hoard of enemies that descended on them. Most of the Yellow Hive's Soldiers were still on top of the plateau, falling over each other in their desire to attack our Queen.

One person was still up there.

Even from this distance, I could smell it was Gil.

He peered over the edge. Our Queen was scuttling toward the line of ships where Lexis and I stood, her path being cut by her few remaining fighters.

Gil nodded and turned back toward the enemies all

around him.

Light flashed in his hands.

The entire plateau erupted in fire, as the explosions we had carefully laid to bring down the pass and secure our escape blew up at once. I ducked back under the rail of the ship I was standing on, gripping it above my head and bracing for the impact.

Good work, Hivemate Gil. You are honored to die for our Queen.

Sound thumped into me, with a huge layer of dust and debris. Some of the debris was bug parts, raining down everywhere. Most of it was tiny rocks, and I buried my head in my hands until the thunder subsided and I could peer over the edge.

Me and all the bugs were scent-blinded by the dust in the air. I could barely see from where I was, but there were enough humans that survived the fighting and the blast to pull the Queen forward, toward the ship where Lexis and I stood.

They needed to get out of here. We all did. But the wind was still blowing, and in what felt like seconds, the air cleared enough for the bugs to start smelling their way around again.

I raced to the edge. "Take her out of here!" I yelled over. "Get her through the pass!"

The people below me heard, and tried to change the Queen's course. With a rush of relief I recognized my dad among them. He didn't look good. One of his arms was hanging at an odd angle, and he wasn't walking right. But he was down there, and he was moving.

"We're coming!" I shouted, but the Queen wouldn't be

swayed.

She kept moving straight toward our ship.

"No, don't come up here! We'll all be trapped!"

Maybe they thought we had more bombs, but we were totally out. If we didn't get down fast, we'd all die.

It was already too late.

The enemy Soldiers swarmed around the base of the ship. Our people and our Queen skittered up the sides, pushing each other and helping the weak. The Queen appeared on top and I reached down to pull my dad up. One of the bugs at the bottom broke away from the group, streaking back toward the Slave Hive. I was sure it was one of ours. *Probably the only one of us that will survive the day.*

We spread out around the edges of the ship, beating down at the enemies that tried to make the climb. In the center sat the Queen, looking serene and calm. I followed her gaze.

She was pointed straight back toward the Slave Hive, and her feelers waved, pulling scent into her flat nostrils.

"What is it?" I asked her, but of course she couldn't understand me.

I picked up a loose bit of the rail that had fallen off and whacked at the head of a Soldier that appeared over the edge. The crunch made me grin.

Behind me, the Queen was still sitting like she hadn't a care in the world, facing the ocean. Her scent matched that far-off water. Blue and smooth.

She knows we're gonna die. She's at peace with it.

I swung my railing at another Soldier. We could hold out here for a bit longer. But their numbers would win the day.

The Queen obviously knew it, too. She turned her eyeless face toward me and clicked a single word in the language Noah had been teaching her.

"Death."

"I think so, too," I told her in human language, and turned back toward the rail. "But I'm not going alone."

CHAPTER 44

NOAH

In the chamber beyond, the Digger stood frozen. Even the paralyzed Soldier stopped moving when I emerged through the crumbling crack from the Queen's chamber, clutching her severed head under my arm.

The boys were still there, standing on wobbly legs.

I clicked to the Digger and the twins. "Come. Follow."

They all did.

I strode up the tunnels, exuding the hated smell of the Hive Queen. Diggers and Builders shrank away as I passed, confused by the scent of their Queen mixed with the scent of death. We emerged into the light.

In the distance I could hear the battle raging. The rest of the escaped humans were long gone. I couldn't see them over the hillside, but surely they'd made it far enough away that the remaining Soldiers wouldn't find them. They'd be safe once they reached the height and cold of the mountain. Our people would find them and lead them to sanctuary.

Explosions ripped the air.

That had to be their escape, the final blast that would bring down the mountain pass. Any minute now, the Hive's Soldiers would be heading my way.

"Whatever happens, you have to get away," I said to the boys stumbling along behind me. I pointed to the pass where Chen would have taken the rest. "Go that way, as fast as you can. Keep running. When you see the feral humans, go with them."

They nodded. They'd learned what the Hive meant. Like me, they knew our lives were lies.

Diggers and Builders crowded around me, and I clutched the Queen's head, machete raised. Along with the boys, I ran toward the ledge that overlooked the long grassy hillside that led to the Forbidden Zone.

The mountain pass stood. I smelled pollen and dead enemy Soldiers by the hundreds. I smelled humans, some alive and some not. I smelled the blue of our Queen.

They hadn't escaped. They were trapped.

"Go!" I screamed at the boys, and took off at a run toward the battle zone. If my Queen died today, I would die by her side.

Sunshine met me at the top of the slope that led down into the Forbidden Zone.

"Bad," he clicked. "Death." He touched the dead Queen's head under my arm and pulled back in alarm.

I could smell it everywhere. Death.

It would be over soon. All our remaining people had climbed to the top of one of the transports. My Queen was there, and Kinni, and Lexis. I could pick out their scents. The wind shifted away from me as I ran but I could still see them, swinging their weapons at the Soldiers that swarmed up the sides, pelting them with arrows that would soon run out.

The Soldiers all around the transport smelled the change in the air. I was suddenly upwind. With their dead Queen's head.

They froze, antennae waving toward me. Our people knocked the highest ones straight off the edge of the transport.

I stopped running and raised the dead Queen's head.

"Death!" I clicked, with fierce, manic joy.

The wind shifted again, and I smelled my Queen's summons. Blue tinged with green, she called me with an urgency I'd never felt.

But my legs were wobbly. I was out of steam.

"My Queen!" I called, stumbling forward.

Strong claws picked me up. Sunshine flung me onto his back and dashed forward toward the tail end of the transport. My machete fell to the ground as I clung on with one hand, gripping the dead head with the other. We pounded toward the ship where the Soldiers were starting to move, no longer stunned by the smell of death in the changing wind.

They swarmed toward us.

We'll never make it. They're right on top of us.

Sunshine slid to a halt and I tumbled off his back. My body skidded right under a crushed section of the transport and I hauled myself up, wedging into a hole in the ship's underbelly. Dragging the Queen's head, I climbed inside the ship.

Outside, Soldiers flung themselves at the thick metal walls. Far ahead, they darted into the half-open hatchway, frenzied at the smell of their dead Queen in my hands.

I lunged forward and jumped onto the interior ladder. Holding the head by its limp antennae, I climbed for my life. I didn't even know why I was still holding it, but couldn't imagine dropping it when I'd come so close.

At the top of the ship, a hatchway was half caved in. I pounded on it, clinging to the ladder as Soldiers rushed toward me inside the ship. The seats below me filled with clicking anger and waving, venomous tails.

With a great, squealing screech of metal, the hatchway above me curled back, ripped away by a great claw. Blue sky shone down, and the massive claw reached in. I grabbed it with one arm, still clutching the head, and it hauled me clear just as the Soldiers launched themselves from the seats below my feet, wordlessly screaming their rage.

I slid onto the top of the transport. From beneath me, the angry clicks of Soldiers echoed inside the ship, but they were too large to fit through the hatch. The hull vibrated as more enemies climbed up the sides.

This is it.

This is where we die.

But we had done it. Chen and the rest of our people were free. Whether or not they found a way to survive on their own in this hostile, bug-ridden wasteland was up to them, as it should have been all along.

And she was here. My glorious Queen.

She settled down next to me and gently took the dead Queen's head from my grasp.

The Soldiers were seconds away.

We didn't have clicks to mean "Goodbye," so I bade my Queen farewell in the only words we had.

"Eat well."

She did.

In five sickening, crunchy bites, she ate the dead Queen's head.

All around us, time stopped.

The enemy Soldiers that had been poised to end our little revolution stopped in their tracks, feelers waving in the air.

My Queen stood up on her hind legs. She exuded her clean, healthy blue scent. The air filled with the joy of her youth and strength, mixed with the yellow of her vanquished enemy.

Every 'Mite, ours and theirs, dropped to their bellies in submission.

The Queen lowered her head, presenting it to me. In awe and wonder, I pulled myself up to my knees and touched the oil she granted, rubbing it onto my skin. First of the hundreds around me to receive her blessing.

First of the new Hive.

The Queen was dead.

Long live the Queen.

CHAPTER 45

NOAH

We sat in the glow of sunset, listening to the waves crash onto the shore. Our Queen perched on the highest rock, antenna sweeping the air. She loved the salty breeze.

Kinni and Lexis trudged up from the beach, each carrying a basket of shellfish. Kinni brought the basket to her dad, who sat next to me in the orange glow.

Mo hadn't fared well in the battle. His right arm caught a stinger full on, and the wound festered. Now there was just a stump where a Builder had nipped the dying arm clean off, crushing the blood vessels with its huge mandibles and saving Mo's life.

Sunshine had also lost a leg when the Soldiers attacked him at the transport. But Lexis had made a wooden replacement, strapping it onto the remnant. Sunshine would limp forever, but would never want for anything. He was the hero of the battle. I grinned, imagining how we must have looked as I rode Sunshine through the battlefield, the dead Queen's head raised like a beacon.

"Cooked or raw?" Lexis asked, jiggling the shellfish in the basket.

"Cooked." Chen answered for all of us.

He had led the people right up to meet our sentries in the mountain pass, just as I knew he would. When the fight ended and our Queen took over the Hive, we sent the least-damaged of our people up to join them. They had been cold and terrified, but in the weeks since the big Hive became our home again, they had settled into their new lives. Some of the women were having a hard time with the real story of our history on the planet, and Kinni rolled her eyes at their insistence that we were all just waiting to get some kind of magical wings. Now the 'Mites that used to be their Masters and our enemies were enemies no longer.

They were hers. Ours. Mine.

Most of the humans didn't live inside the giant mound. Along with the 'Mites, we had started building our own, individual homes, scattered around the ridge. The Hive was becoming a city. None of us wanted to live inside the place that had been our prison.

Our Queen didn't want to, either.

Lexis was starting to sort out the normal biology of these insects. She had already guessed some of it. When a Queen egg was laid, it was supposed to be allowed to hatch. If the existing Queen was healthy, the new one would leave the Hive with a group of Diggers and Builders, and go off to found her own Hive far from the old one. Now we knew that if the old Queen was ailing, the new Queen would stay in the original Hive, kill the old Queen, and eat her head, taking over the Hive and all the 'Mites that lived in it. In this Hive, that hadn't happened for far too long.

We trooped down to gather around an open fire on the beach. Most of the 'Mites stayed away from the fire, retiring to their normal places in the dark tunnels. But the ones that had fought with us, that had come to serve our Queen in the distant, ruined mound, they stayed out with all the humans.

The last of the sun dipped below the horizon, and stars began to twinkle as darkness overcame the sky. We sat around the fire, cooking our evening meal.

Lexis had figured it out.

In the weeks after the battle, she combed every inch of the Hive, searching for whatever it was that made the humans of the Hive able to bond with the Queen through her oil. She tried the fungus that grew in the dark gardens underground, but it didn't work. She drank the water that flowed in our river, but it was the same water that came down from the high mountain peaks and coursed under the whole area. I took her into all the dark chambers, and she breathed deeply, suspecting some spore in the air here.

In the end, it was the waterbugs.

"You eat them raw?" She'd been aghast. "They've got to be full of parasites. Who knows what all. You have to cook them through."

I demonstrated, crushing one of the wiggling bugs with a rock, and scraping out the translucent, jelly meat inside. "You just slurp it down. They're really good." I nodded at Kinni. "They're her absolute favorite."

Kinni pretend-gagged. "They're horrible."

Lexis held her nose and took a bite. "Disgusting." She

gagged, but held it down. Her brow furrowed and she peered at Kinni.

"You've eaten these things raw?"

A shrug from Kinni. "He dared me."

"When?"

I thought about it. "After you all came back down the mountain. Before we found all the weapons in the transport."

We had carried the rest up and cooked them in the fire. Even I had to admit they were a lot better when cooked. Lexis touched the oil from the Queen's head as she did every night, making notes in her little book about what she'd done that day.

Nothing happened for three days. But on the morning of the fourth day, after Lexis had received the oil again, she woke me from a sound sleep.

"Noah! Do you smell that? It's blue!"

I grinned. "Yes, it's blue. Like the sea on a bright day. The Queen is happy this morning."

She thought it must be a parasite. Something that incubated in the waterbugs, and lived in the brains of the 'Mites, and in us. Something that responded to the pheromones in the Queen's oil and changed our brain chemistry, bonding us together.

"It makes perfect sense. They're blind. Smell is everything to them. It's how they communicate, and how she binds us all into one family, one mind." She paused, realizing what she said. "Us. I'm part of it now. I'm part of the Hive."

I had laughed. "We're all part of the Hive."

We ate our dinner, watching the sky fade from purple to black. The fire shot sparks up to the stars.

Along with our Diggers, we were planting some of the seeds we'd found in the transports. If we were lucky, we'd soon have plants growing that had come from a distant planet. Where we'd come from.

"Show me again where Earth was?" I asked Mo.

He pointed into the eastern sky. "It was there." His finger traced a long, serpentine row of stars. "The one at the end." It was dim in the cloudy sky.

I took a pile of raw shellfish to the Queen. She received them graciously, emitting a warm scent of appreciation. I wished humans had the ability to share our feelings through our scents the way our Hivemate 'Mites could. We would always need the clicking language to help them understand us, and our own language to communicate with each other. But everyone in the Hive knew our Queen's devotion to us.

She was as different from the old Yellow Queen as the ocean was from the moons. I liked to think the fact that she had shared blood with me in her larval form somehow let her see humans as part of her Hive, as valued as 'Mites. She still didn't speak a lot of the clicking language, but she didn't have to. Her scent told us everything we needed to know about her wants and moods, and every human and 'Mite in the Hive would give their life to protect her. Our Queen was serene in the starlight, confident and benevolent. I breathed in her scent and thought about the story the women of the Hive had told. Over the years, the real tale of Horizon Beta's flight from another planet was twisted and warped. The women believed that when we were worthy, we would get wings. As I reveled in the closeness of my Hive, I realized they were right. In the safety of my family, I was a winged dragonfly, soaring over a perfect blue ocean.

The old Hive's King sat uneasily next to the Queen. The only true male in the Hive, he would soon be the father of all the eggs our Queen would lay. He hated being out in the open air, but she refused to accompany him down into the dark chamber where her predecessor had lived. No deep tunnels for the Queen that had been hatched in sunlight. He'd have to get used to it.

And no more seals. In my flight from this Hive that seemed a hundred years ago, I'd stumbled on the answer. Our vats of algae, brought down from the stars, were a perfect nourishment for 'Mite eggs and larvae. We'd started making large clay vessels so that when the Queen was ready to lay eggs, each one could have its own supply.

Kinni helped her dad open a shell, scooping out the hot meat. She settled down next to him and looked up toward the wash of stars overhead. "I wonder if they would have sent us here if they'd known."

I looked around at the faces reflected in the firelight. Humans and insects, one Hive together, content and safe on a sandy beach.

"Probably not," I said. "But of all those stars they could have picked, they found us the perfect place. I think we're going to make it just fine."

I lay back on the warm sand, smelling the salt breeze and the contentment of my Hive.

The people of the Horizon Beta were home.

If you loved

Horizon Beta,

don't miss the adventures of the passengers of the other
ships that left earth,

Horizone Alpha and *Horizon Delta!*

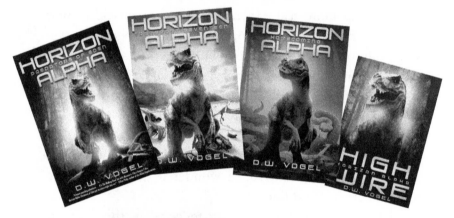

Horizon Delta
Coming:
September 2020

FHP

NEVER MISS A FUTURE HOUSE RELEASE!

Sign up for the Future House Publishing email list:
www.futurehousepublishing.com/beta-readers-club

www.facebook.com/FutureHousePublishing

www.twitter.com/FutureHousePub

www.youtube.com/FutureHousePublishing

www.instagram.com/FutureHousePublishing

ACKNOWLEDGMENTS

Folks who don't write might imagine a book like this springing forth, fully formed, from a solitary person sitting in front of a computer, wrapped in a blanket and covered in cats. While the computer and cat part is absolutely true, and the blanket part is seasonally accurate, there's nothing solitary about the process of bringing a manuscript from rough draft to publication. I owe the success of this story to the unsung heroes of the book world:

To my husband, Andrew, who listens to idea after idea as the story takes shape in my mind.

To my faithful first readers, Jude Rose and Nik Everhart, who ask all the right questions.

To my series science advisor, Joe Childers, who keeps the Horizon fleet flying.

To my entomology advisor, May Berenbaum, who made the 'Mites real.

To my editorial team; Emma, Abbie, and Stephanie; who comb through draft after draft, shining up the Hive.

To my agent, Alice Speilburg, who believes in all my worlds.

You are my Soldiers, my Diggers, and my Builders. Long live the Horizon Hive.

ABOUT THE AUTHOR

D. W. Vogel is a veterinarian, marathon runner, cancer survivor, SCUBA diver, and current president of Cincinnati Fiction Writers. She is the author of the *Horizon Arc* from Future House Publishing, the fantasy novel *Flamewalker*, and the writing manual *Five Minutes to Success: Master the Craft of Writing*. She also has short stories in several anthologies from various publishers.

Wendy loves to hear from readers, so feel free to contact her on her website (https://wendyvogelbooks.com/) or on Twitter (https://twitter.com/drwendyv).

WANT D. W. VOGEL TO COME TO YOUR SCHOOL?

What makes a hero? Wendy has visited schools and museums to talk with kids about just that. Using Star Wars as an example, she takes a look at the classic Hero's Journey in literature. Ideal for grades 3–6, this is a fun introduction into the interpretation of story structure. Through the journey of Luke Skywalker, students will learn about courage and motivation, and the altruism that defines a real hero.

For more information visit: http://www.futurehousepublishing.com/authors/d-w-vogel/ Or contact: schools@futurehousepublishing.com

CPSIA information can be obtained
at www.ICGtesting.com
Printed in the USA
BVHW082016130320
575012BV00001B/1